This Game Has NO Loyalty

Part III: Love Is Pain

Written By: June

This book is a work of fiction. Names, character, places and incident are the product of the author's imagination or are used fictitiously. Any resemblance to actual events, locals or persons, living or dead is purely coincidental.

Editor: Thomas Hill – Launchpad Press

Printed in the United States of America

First Edition

ISBN#: 13-digit: 978-0-9827679-2-4
10-digit: 0-9827-6792-7

Published by: FourShadough Publishing, LLC

This Game Has NO Loyalty

Part III: Love Is Pain

FOUR SHADOUGH
PUBLISHING

Acknowledgements

The ability to write stories that touches the masses or just one person is one of the greatest rewards of being an author. I have experienced and learned so much during this literary journey and I want to thank God for this gift he has bestowed on me to write creative and compelling stories that many of my readers enjoy and relate to. There are so many people to thank on this project and so many that deserve acknowledgements. If I forget anyone, please know that it is not intentional and I will shout you out on my next project.

Mom, without the love you have consistently showered me with, I would have never been able to focus enough to finish this project, which has taken me much too long to complete. Your faith in my abilities has pushed me to the apex. I love you and am grateful you have stood by me in my darkest times.

Nate, you have been such an inspiration in my life and if I don't say it enough, I love you man! I cherish our relationship, although we are brothers, you are my best friend. I look forward to our talks and leave each conversation learning something new from you. Thanks for being such a great brother and friend. It's your turn!

Donnell (D-Boy), our friendship is priceless my dude. We are still growing and in our maturity we have shown that true friendship is a gift not to be taken for granted. We have experienced almost every adversity life has presented and rose to the top like cream. I'm proud to see how we made the transformation from boys to men to fathers!

Ramel, many don't understand your wisdom because you give freely and without prejudice. You have always given me great advice and always praised me when I needed to hear it most. Our years of friendship have proven that even friends have disagreements but real friends won't let any disagreement stand in the way of their friendship. This is called "Ole skool friendship". You are my brother from another mother.

Sha-Juan (first born daughter), babygirl, your daddy loves you tremendously. You are a very intelligent and bright young lady and I'm very proud of all your accomplishments. I know you are getting older baby and your daddy sees and understands your growth into a young, respectable teenager. You must remember that you are a young lady with an independent mind. You should never subject yourself to peer pressure because your last name is Miller and you are a leader not a follower. I have supreme confidence in you and I love you with every chamber of my heart.

Shaaid (first born son), my little man who I cherish. You are such a little comedian. You are so witty with your words and have such a magnetic personality. I want you to remember that you are leader and not a follower. Keep improving with your academic studies and I'll meet you at the top my young soldier. I love you Po.

Shadiya (2nd born daughter), daddy's precious angel. You have so much character and intelligence at your age. You are a remarkable little girl with so much respect and love for your family that some adults need to learn this from you. Nu Nu, you are such a special girl and daddy loves you dearly.

Shamel (2nd born son), Man Man, you are in daddy's likeness. I can see your success permeating through your solid character. You amaze everyone who meets you and leave an impression on their hearts that they will not soon forget. I love you so much and know your success is already cemented through me.

Peaches, you have remained such a good friend throughout our lifelong friendship. You have always voiced your opinions sincerely and although we don't agree on everything and see eye-to-eye at times that has not tarnished the relationship we have. Thank you for being real at all times.

Eva Gray (Eva Keyes), you are my sister and my best friend. Our relationship grew from the "blue house" and we have maintained our alliance throughout the years. I cherish your words of wisdom and your medical advice. You know you're my private nurse. I am proud of you and know you are proud of me because we've always wanted the best for each other. You are my peeps for life.

Michele, I must thank you for the obvious changes I've made in my life that only people that have known me in my prior life can see. Your presence and your kind caring words in my times of despair is what helped me complete this project. Your input and constant interest in the most microscopic details of this project is what kept me focused and got me to the finish line. For that I love and thank you.

Shaneda, how can I thank you? You have lifted me up with your words on numerous occasions when I was literally ready to give this all up. Your unselfish ways is what separates you from the rest of the world. I commend you on the accomplishments and the same way you have pushed me, I will be in your corner whenever you need that pep talk or push when times get a little hard as it sometimes does. Thank you for having my back Neda, you are the best!

Cuwan, (Cue), I expect so much from you and I know that you will surprise the world and become successful. You are such a smart dude and you have begun to move with better intentions. This Game Has no Loyalty and Love is Pain, you have experienced this first hand. Remember that wisdom is gained by applying knowledge. Keep your head up and your feet planted firm and move with a purpose my son. Love you.

Chanae (Nay Nay), baby girl, you have grown up to be such a smart and beautiful young woman. You are learning and I hope you don't rob yourself of what's rightfully yours. The sky's the limit so don't become complacent. The world is at your disposal, all your dreams will come true but it will take hard work. I am proud of you so continue to move in the right direction. I will see you when you reach the top.

Mark (Marky Mark), I see the change in you. You have gotten so mature and have become so responsible in such a short time that it's like you're another person. I am so very proud of your accomplishments and how focused you are. You are learning a lot of things but you must remain consistent with how you deal with difficult things you don't understand. I am here for you when you feel no one will/can understand. Your success is a given so forget reaching for the stars, reach for the sun because your future is bright.

Dina (Sis), they say great minds think alike. I love you sis and I know all you do is going to turn out the way you want. I want to thank you for always being there for me whenever I needed to bend your ear. Your advice kept me grounded and made me make the logical choices in my life. Love you.

Cakez, I just want you to know that you are a great mother, person, and friend. You are the kind of woman that many women should aspire to become. You faced the most difficult times and never once did you give up, you kept pushing and stayed focus. I applaud you for your strong character and your remarkable abilities in the wake of issues most would fold under. 22 is our number.

Shout outs: Detail (Chee Chi), Stubbs, D-Nice, Billy Bang, Mizzo, 1100, Uncle D, Greg (Gee), Donna, 99, Shrimpo, Crazy Ty, Shabazz, B.Z., Kiffy Boy, Big Moe, Party Rob, Big L, Cecil, Bistro, Darrell, Cliff, Lexus Coupe, Tone Loc, Angel, B Angie B, Black, Bridget, Kenny Kings, Ronnett, Lovely One, Cee, Cheryl, Christina (Cherry), Divine, Tameka, Marsha, Johanna, Dwayne (General), Gloria, Bam (Headrush), Jah, Jay, Artie Art, Jeff, Carla, Kurt Flurt, Shaneka (god daugter), La, Mandy, Nashawn (cuzzo), Shamel, Barry, Nikia, Pantha, Supreme, Pocahantas, Rachel, Sam (sister), Rhonda Crowder, Sexy, Renee, Spoonie Rock, Toni (S.C.), Twan, Troy, Wanda, Willie, Kim, Deborah Cardona (Sexy), Kisha Greene (Keesh), Nikiesha Grant, Carla Dean, Dashawn Taylor, Lachanda, Tyesha, K'wan, Erick Gray, Carmen, Darlene, Dawn Champion, English Ruler, SiStar Tea, Glenda, Joe Centeno, Trina Daniels, Agnes, Yolanda Parker, Kamilah, Cliff Boston, Raleek, Mark, Nancy Lopez, Sabrina, Saquan, Shameek, Sherry, Tanya, Rellz (Big Sis), Yvonne, Sunshine.

My fam: Miller, Cirilo, Dina, Jannett, Bernadette, Billy, Linda, Li'l Greg, Monique, Yolanda, Yvette, Minerva, Orlando, Kenrick, Valiah, Syira, Emiani, Naphie, Mischell, Rey, Lorna, Jonathan, Peggy, Penny, Junior, Tia, Tia Barbara, Uncle Rich, Uncle Dexter, the entire Miller Clan and all cousins and offsprings.

My L Dub fam: Pat (Cakez), Piff (Diva), Kellz, Gretta, Mikki, Niyoko, Gloria, Angie, Meaka, Liz Clark, Shlanda, Meka Dudley, A.D., Alton (Mr. CEO), Bunky, Steve Windley, Steve Gorham, Damon, Lewis A., Alton O., Ronnie S., Ricky, Darrel, Dawan, Baseball, Godfather Kurt, Chubby, Hank, Tabu, Stickman, Ziggy, Bink (Beanie), Fruit, Al Green, Shawn, Damian, Li'l Dee, Donald (Sleepy), Jerome, Bolo, Katrina, Kee Kee, Rat, Bathsheba, B.J., Darryl Leathers, Keith, Ant Smallwood, Angela Wilson, Sharia, Lance, Latasha, Aimee Parker, Lateese, Marcus Miller, Stacy Keech, Vanessa, Veronica, Wanda.

Special Thanks: Novel Tees, Urban Book Source, Hood Novels, Philly Horizon Books, Cartel Café Bookstore, Coast 2 Coast, Bronx Bookman, DC Bookdiva, OOSA Book Club

DEDICATIONS

I must dedicate this work to my comrade, my best friend, my A-alike, my fam, ERIC JEROME KEECH. He left us much too early and is sorely missed. In his death I keep his memory alive by belting out these stories in hopes one young male will read and interpret the true meaning of living life. I also dedicate this work to his son Jahiem whom I regretfully admit that I have not spoken to in some time but will change that after the completion of this project. Jahiem is bright, athletic, studious, and a success driven young man. I am very proud of him and his mother Mikki who has held him down remarkably. God has blessed you both.

Black (Eric), I miss you so much man. Not a day goes by that I don't think about you and the times we shared. I remember the talks we had, the growth in the ten + years we've been homies and what I miss most is your laugh. You were the Mayor of Li'l Washington, you gave that town energy and when you left some of that energy went along with you. Everyone that met you loved you.

RIP

RIP: Jo Jo Albritton, Kirk, Eugene Battle, Terrence Gray, Tyran (8-Ball), Rasheen (Ra Dolla), Kaseem

Chapter 1
****La****

La dipped into the store when the police car stopped in the middle of the street. The police officer never saw him because his concentration was on the car Junior and Muffin were in that was wrapped around the fire hydrant. When the police car sped down the block chasing after Junior and Muffin, La calmly left the store then headed back to Baptiste. He was enraged because he missed his chance to get his revenge on Junior, although Rock hadn't been as lucky. He passed police cars parked on the sidewalk blocking the entrance to the lane that led to the back of the building. The police weren't allowing anyone entry through, so he walked around to the front then crossed the street and joined the crowd that had gathered to find out what happened in the back of the building.

Shondra sat on a bench while a female officer asked her questions about what happened.

"I told you, I think the bitch name was Buffy or some shit!" Shondra was telling the officer.

"You said she had a gun. Did the guy with her have a gun too?" the officer questioned.

“YES!” Shondra confirmed.

“Would you be able to identify both of them if we brought you down to look through our mug book?” the officer asked.

“YES!”

Taylor and Burke walked away with a loaded gun found on the scene. Ballistics removed the slug that was trapped inside the steel door. They were walking back to their car when Taylor stopped abruptly.

“Hold on, partner, look who’s sitting over there on the benches and it looks like she’s giving a statement,” Taylor told his partner, Burke.

“Say no more, this might be the break we were looking for,” Burke said, walking in Shondra’s direction.

“Hello again. Ms. Brown, is it?” Taylor asked, walking up to Shondra.

“Yes, how you doin’?” Shondra replied. Taylor looked at the female officer and by his look she knew he wanted privacy and walked off with the information she already obtained from Shondra.

“I’m fine, the question is are you? Did you get caught up in the mess back here?” Taylor asked nicely.

“Yep.” She responded flatly.

“If you don’t mind, can I ask you a couple questions? I mean, if you’re up to it,” Taylor asked her.

“Ask away, I don’ told that lady everything. I don’t give a fuck no more,” Shondra said, folding her arms across her bosom.

“Well then, do you mind telling me what happened back here?” Taylor asked.

“OK look, I told her one time already and I don’t feel like going through the whole shit again. If you want to

ask the same questions, get them from her because I got a fuckin' headache from all this bullshit!"

"Okay, Ms. Brown, just one question. Do you know the names of anyone that had anything to do with what happened here today?" Taylor pushed.

"Junior…Junior and Muffy…I think that's his bitch name!" She stood up and walked away. She just realized what she'd done, if Junior found out she snitched on him, he would never fuck with her again. Taylor looked down at the evidence bag that contained the handgun they found near the back of the building.

"You think…?" Taylor began, looking at his partner and the evidence bag containing the shell casing from the back door of the building.

"I hope so, partner. Let's go get this evidence processed ourselves and run the prints," Burke said, heading to their patrol car.

As the detectives walked to their car, Chico sat at a window looking down at what was going on. He didn't want his name involved in anything because it would mean bad news for him if he were to be picked up and La found out about it.

La watched as Shondra walked toward him with her head lowered. She was crying so he walked over to her before she entered her building.

"Yo, what's up Shondra?" he asked.

Shondra was startled when she turned and saw La standing right behind her. Like most people in the hood, she thought he died that day in the back of the building with Drez.

"What's up, Lakim?" she said, calling him by his full God body name.

"Nuthin'. I know, everybody thought I was dead," he replied, having an idea what she was thinking when she

saw him. "I feel like a ghost. Yo, what dem pigs was talkin' 'bout over there?"

"Trying to see what I know but I told them I didn't know shit. I was out there 'bout to…" she started, but then the thought of what Muffin did came back to her and she began talking loosely without thinking. "You know that muhfucka had the nerve to bring that dirty bitch around here after I don' went through mad shit wit' him over her!"

"Who you talkin' 'bout, Shondra?" La asked with interest.

"Junior and that bitch he fuckin' with," she bellowed.

"Word? That's fucked up, that's some real slimy shit. I thought you and him were still together?" La said.

"Yea, my dumb ass thought the same thing too. Looks like I'm the asshole. Then the bitch had the nerve to pull out on me and robbed me for my fuckin' shines." Shondra was waving her hand in a gesture to show her missing diamond ring.

"Get the fuck outta here. She pulled a gat on you? Whoa! That's foul for real. You think he set you up for that?" La instigated.

"He brung the bitch didn't he? If he didn't know, he still gets charged for being a dirty muhfucka!"

"Damn Shondra, that's really fucked up. I didn't know you was going through that shit. But check it: if you want to get back at that muhfucka let me know. I know you heard he tried to murk me a while back," La told her. That's when it came to her; she remembered what Junior told her about what happened in the back of the building. How La tried to set him up by using another guy who happened to be Muffin's cousin. She didn't want to get mixed up with any extra drama, so she played it safe.

"I heard about that," she admitted to him.

"I'm good now but it's fucked up how he just flipped on me like that. I think it was over something a bitch told him about me that wasn't true; I don't even know the bitch that told him that shit! It's probably the same bitch that just pulled out on you. I think the whole time the bitch was trying to take over. She gonna bring him down so you shouldn't even sweat that bullshit," La said to her.

"You know something, La? You right! Fuck him and that fake ass squeaky voice bitch!" Shondra said in agreement.

"I hear that," La responded.

"Aight La, I'm going in the crib, I'll talk with you."

"Cool, see you later, Shondra. Don't forget what I said. I'm right across the street." La walked away and waited for the police to take down the yellow tape then went into the building where he knew Chico's scared ass would be.

***

The knock on the door startled Chico while he was looking out the window watching the last of the NYPD units disperse. He tipped over to the door and looked through the peephole but couldn't see anything but blackness. Then the door shook.

"Open the fucking door!" Chico unlocked the deadbolt nervously. As La pushed the door open, Chico backed up, his eyes fixed on the gun in La's hand.

"Wha…wha…what up, La?" he stuttered.

La looked at him with disgust. "What the fuck happened out there!"

"If you talking 'bout with Junior, he hit me with a gun. He think I'm fuckin' his girl," Chico said, nursing his wound.

La cocked his head to the side. "Are you?" he asked.

"I fucked her a couple times but she the one that pressed me," Chico claimed.

La started laughing and thought to himself, "*That's a slick bitch. She flippin' on Junior and she fuckin' this faggot-ass dude*." La holstered the pistol in his waist then walked into the kitchen and sat down staring at Chico.

"You scared of that dude, ain't you?" La asked Chico.

"I ain't scared of him. He pulled a biscuit and snuffed me with it. If he wanted to fight straight up, we woulda locked ass," Chico responded.

"Is *that* right? So you scared of guns?" La looked at him with a strange gleam in his eye.

"Hell yea, I ain't tryin' to get shot!" Chico said.

"You scared of the wrong thing. You shouldn't be scared of guns 'cause they don't shoot by themselves." La pulled his gun out and pointed it at Chico. "You better be scared of the muhfucka behind the ratchet." Chico put his hands up to his face trying to cover up, "Ay chill, La."

"You scared of me or the gun?" La asked menacingly.

"Please La, don't do this man." Chico begged.

"YOU SCARED OF ME OR THIS GUN, I SAID!" La screamed.

"YOU, I'm scared of you, please La!"

La's eyes were bloodshot and big as saucers. His blood was pumping like water through a fire hose as he lowered the gun slowly. He wanted to savor the feeling of

fear he imposed on Chico. It was beginning to consume him and he was enjoying the power he now possessed.

"Straighten up and listen. That shit that just went down today, it can't happen again, you hear me?" La sneered. Chico breathed out a sigh of relief as his heart rate slowed down to a normal pace. "Yea man, I hear you."

"Aight, now check it. This shit ain't over, I gotta take that muhfucka out now 'cause he seen me. This is life or death beef," La said through clenched teeth.

"What you want me to do?" Chico asked perplexed.

"I'ma need you to find out where this muhfucka be at. I don't care where you get it but get it. Since you fucking his girl, see if you can find something out from her. I already know he hang out in Tompkins with his cousin but he strong out there, I need to catch his ass away from his hang out. Matter of fact, get her to tell you where that bitch he fucking with live. She should be glad to tell you that," La suggested.

"I don't think she gon' give up no information like that to me. She don't talk about him to me like that," Chico said.

"She will. After you finishing fucking just bring it up, it's called pillow talk, muhfucka, so just find out and I'm not asking you Chico, I'm telling you." La gave an ice-cold look to Chico.

Chico gave in. "Aight La, I'll try and find out what I can for you."

Knocking over the chair he was sitting in, La rushed over to Chico and stood nose to nose with him. He could smell the fear as he whispered into his ear with cyanide-laced words, "Don't try…do it!"

"Aight La." Chico was shaking from fear.

Chico stepped back and looked at La. He didn't know La's background and from what he heard from the hood, La was a cool dude but that's not what he was seeing. La was like a madman. La was taking advantage of him by imposing fear to make him do his bidding. It was becoming too much for Chico to bear and he was walking on eggshells every time he was around La. He was being forced to dig his own grave by getting information from Shondra about her man, who just pistol-whipped him because he thought they were fucking around. It was going to take something short of a miracle for him to be able to walk away from all this with his life. He didn't sign up for this when he started hustling and never thought he would be exposed to the kind of bullshit he was facing. Life for him would never be the same.

******Junior******

Junior was running a hot bath for Muffin while she lay on her bed, sore from the car accident. He was sitting on the edge of the rectangular porcelain tub, periodically sticking his hand under the water to feel the temperature. He peeked in on Muffin who was holding a wet cloth to her head, rocking back and forth on the bed.

"Don't go to sleep, baby" he yelled to her from the bathroom.

"I'm not daddy but my head is killing me. Go downstairs and get me some Tylenol outta the kitchen draw please!" she screamed back to him.

"Aight, just don't go to sleep, Muff," he said, walking out of the room. Muffin's mother was in the kitchen cooking when Junior entered. He usually avoided

her at all costs because he wasn't big on the Q & As most girls' mothers wanted to ask their daughter's boyfriend.

"Hey, Mr. Man," she said to Junior as she put a lid on a silver pot that was steaming on the stove.

"Hi, how you doin', Ms. Turner?" Junior replied.

"Where's Charlene?" she asked, stirring another pot.

"She's upstairs lying down. I came down here to get her a Tylenol," Junior responded.

"Oh, she has a headache?" Ms. Turner said. It was that time of the month when women felt under the weather.

"Yea. Um, how was your day?" Junior asked her.

"It was fine, just fine. Thanks for asking." Ms. Turner appreciated his gesture because no one, not even Muffin, ever asked her how her day went. "Let me get that Tylenol for you."

"Thank you." Junior looked at Ms. Turner as she pulled out the drawer and searched for a Tylenol. She had on a blue polyester skirt with a matching one-button blazer that fit her snug. The dark-colored sheer stockings she had on showed her thick thighs and calf muscles, which made her legs look like a champion racing horse. Junior's eyes were glued to her Coke bottle-shaped body and they roamed from her round apple ass to her powerful sexy legs. When she turned around he tried to look away but she caught him looking, and in that instant she became a little warm.

"Thank you, Ms. Turner," he said, quickly taking the pack of Tylenol out of her hand and leaving the kitchen.

"Do you want some dinner, Junior?" she asked him before he left the kitchen.

"Huh?" he answered, turning around to face her.

"I said do you want some dinner. I'm making baked turkey wings and rice with steamed broccoli."

"Um…sure," he replied, staring into her hazel eyes.

"Ask Muffin if she feels well enough to come down, if not I'll make a plate for you to take to her upstairs, OK?" She said turning back around and tending to the steaming pots.

"Sure, Ms. Turner. Thanks again," he replied.

Junior walked up the stairs to give Muffin her Tylenol. Ms. Turner watched him as he walked away and had the most impure thoughts about him. It had been so long since she had a shot of some dick that she was allowing her estrogen to control her thinking. Junior was her daughter's boyfriend but he was stocky and looked as sturdy as a tree trunk, his skin was clear and tight, and he looked like his zipper was caging an anaconda behind it. Her body began to react to her thoughts, her middle got moist and she leaned up against one of the high chairs positioned by the counter and rubbed her front on the cushion slowly, as her mind was invaded by tainted thoughts of bedding down her daughter's boyfriend.

She imagined him grabbing her from behind and massaging her breasts and grinding on her soft ass then she started to move her body to her thoughts. Closing her eyes, she put her hands on her breasts and squeezed gently. She was totally submerged in her fantasy and it felt as if he was really behind her grinding and rubbing her hips and thighs. She threw her head back and felt his balmy breath on her neck and invited the warmth, her eyes still closed.

Her passion escalated because she needed to be satisfied erotically, sexually, and emotionally so she moved back, letting the feeling take over. Her mind was so powerfully emerged into her desire that she was physically

feeling his presence. She turned around and could smell his cologne as if he were standing there with her. She put her tongue in his mouth and kissed him passionately as her kitty kat pulsated and throbbed. She felt his hands lifting her skirt and she felt him rip her pantyhose in the middle so he could finger her sticky middle. She moaned as she continued kissing him, spreading her legs apart to give him access to her hub. Her body jerked when his finger entered and she bit down on his tongue gently. His finger went in deeper and moved in a circular motion, searching for a tender spot to bring her to orgasm.

It had been so long since she had anything other than a tampon inserted into her center that she exploded almost immediately. She shivered and shook as he moved his finger rapidly inside her and she creamed. When the feeling was over she opened her eyes. To her shock, Junior was standing in front of her, live and in person. She pushed him back with both hands to see if it was real. Junior took two steps back and lowered his head, almost in shame. She looked down at her ruined panty hose and pulled her skirt down quickly. She was speechless.

"I came back down to get some water for Muffin. When I came in here you were calling my name then you grabbed me and started kissing me," Junior explained.

"I did what!" Ms. Turner was shocked and embarrassed at the same time. "Oh my God, I can't believe this! This was not supposed to happen, you're my daughter's boyfriend for Christ's sake!"

"Well it happened and I liked it," Junior said slyly, his confidence growing.

"Please, boy!" She pointed and wagged her finger at Junior. "This never happened! And don't tell my baby!" Ms. Turner shook her head. "I can't believe this shit even happened!" The smoke coming from the pots broke her train of thought and she walked over to the stove and turned off the burners then moved the pots to the back of the range with an oven mitt. She turned back around to finish addressing Junior about what happened but Muffin came through the kitchen door.

"Ay, mama" she said, holding a white rag against her forehead.

"Ay, baby. What happened to your head?" Her mother was concerned.

"We had a minor car accident today. Junior ain't tell you?" Muffin asked.

Ms. Turner shot a look at Junior and he shot one back.

"No, he only said you had a headache." She stared daggers at Junior, upset her daughter was hurt and she wasn't informed. "Are you OK, baby?"

"Yea, ma, it's not that serious." She walked over to Junior. "Boy, what is taking you so long to get my doggone water?"

"I was talking to your moms." He looked at Ms. Turner.

"That's all you better had been doing," she said, a smirk appearing on her face. Ms. Turner looked down and noticed her skirt was not pulled all the way down showing the tear in her stockings but the counter was blocking Muffin from seeing that.

"You want something to eat, honey?" she asked, moving further away from Muffin.

"I'm not really hungry. I just came down because this boy act like he had to go up a hill to fetch a pail of water," Muffin said, walking toward the refrigerator.

"I'll get it for you, baby" Ms. Turner said quickly opening the refrigerator.

"OK, thanks…what you standing there looking crazy for, baby?" Muffin turned her attention to Junior. Junior looked at her and answered, "You know I got a lot on my mind. My bad."

"Well I'm glad I wasn't dyin' of thirst or I'd be dead," she said, grabbing Junior's hand.

"Don't say that, baby," her mother said, placing the glass of water on the counter.

"Thanks, ma. Come on, boy" Muffin said, pulling Junior's hand as she walked out of the kitchen. Ms. Turner watched as Junior was dragged by his hand out of the kitchen then placed both hands on the counter and held her head down. She felt terrible about what happened but her body was sending her a different message. She looked up to the ceiling and prayed for the strength not to make the mistake again.

Muffin disrobed when she got into her room and headed for the bathroom.

"You wanna get in with me, daddy?" she asked, feeling the temperature of the water.

"Um, nah, you get in and just relax," Junior replied.

"You sure, baby?" She opened the door revealing her nakedness. "The water is just right." Junior looked at her and got an immediate rise from the view. He was realizing where Muffin got her hourglass shape from and was almost certain her body would look like her mother's when she reached her age.

"Stop playin' girl. I'm gonna go outside and get some air," he told her, getting up to leave the room.

"OK. I'm gonna soak for awhile 'cause my head is really hurting me."

Junior left the bedroom. He was worried the police found the gun he dropped in Baptiste. Once they got his

fingerprints off the gun he was sure there would be a warrant out for his arrest. He needed to find out for sure because his freedom depended on it.

***

When Taylor received the fingerprints back from the evidence that was submitted, he and Burke immediately pulled Junior's file.

"Perfect match! I knew it. I told you, Burke," Taylor remarked with a smile on his face. Burke stood next to his partner and nodded his head in agreement.

"The bullet found on the scene wasn't discharged from the gun we found out there but his prints do match the gun found on the scene. We have a case on possession. That's enough for me and once we get him in custody, we'll have more leverage to get a confession out of him or a lead on one of the murders then we can start closing these fucking murder cases," Taylor said with satisfaction.

"Did you check to see if the weapon was used in any of the unsolved homicides?" Burke asked his partner.

"Right now, nothing has come back from ballistics, but I'm sure we can build a strong enough case to get that maggot off the streets. He got away the last time but he won't get away again," Taylor said defiantly.

"There has been a lot of activity happening in the back of that building. Do you think he had something to do with Rock's murder? Maybe he was over there trying to silence an eyewitness?" Burked guessed.

"I was thinking along those lines. Suppose it's a fight over territory? The guy we found murdered behind that building some months back had drugs near him. We

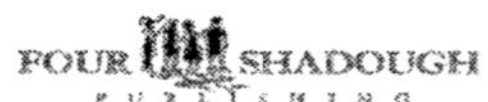

know it's where those guys hustle their drugs; I'm suspecting it's over territory," Taylor emphasized.

"And I'm suspecting you're right," Burke said in agreement.

The two detectives sat down at their desks and began writing notes and pulling files. They were preparing to build a solid case against Junior.

Chapter 2
*** *Shondra****

The cold air whipped through the light leather jacket Chico was wearing, causing him to shiver and push his hands deeper into his pockets. There weren't many people out but it wasn't just due to the drop in temperature, La had turned Baptiste into his personal war zone of sorts. Chico had no idea why La made the beef between him and Junior seem like it was Junior's fault. From what Rock had told him, La was the one that violated and tried to set Junior up; that's how he wound up getting shot. The beef between both men went so deep and was so deadly Chico didn't know how to get out of it because La stuck him in the middle. It seemed La needed his assistance in quenching his thirst for revenge and made it painfully clear he wanted results.

Chico was marked for death by Junior since being forced to sell only La's product in Baptiste and not paying off what was owed from the package Junior had given him. And if that wasn't enough, he was fucking Junior's crazy-ass girl and she was making his life a living hell. Hustling just wasn't as fun as when he worked under Rock. It had

become so serious and the money wasn't worth all the bullshit.

Chico wasn't sure how to get out from under La's reign. He had ideas although none were really feasible. The only realistic thing he could do to get out of it was to kill La. But he wasn't built for the murder game so he was stuck. He would have to play it out and do as he was told to do until he figured a way out. There was a sense of urgency on getting the information La wanted because he had been asking Chico everyday if he had any news for him and like an obsessed maniac, his anger seemed to escalate whenever Chico told him he didn't find out anything.

Chico tried to get information from Shondra but dealing with her was becoming a headache. She was just as mentally abusive as La but on a whole different level. Her disrespect was constant and she treated him like he was a child. She was always trying to tell him what to do with his money, how much to give her, and how much he should save. She made him take her out to eat, to the movies, and clothes shopping almost every two weeks and made a scene if he refused. He had to go to her house every night and if he missed a night she would literally come looking for him and blow his pager up throughout the entire night until he called her back. And if he were foolish enough to call back, she would curse him out like he was the bitch and she was the man.

It didn't stop there; she would come to the back of the building and demand money from him around all the young workers, embarrassing him if he opposed her. He was sick and tired of her; she and La was the worst thing that happened to him and he dreaded ever making their acquaintances. The only reason she was getting away with

her bullshit was because he didn't want to add any more fire to an already hazardous situation with Junior.

Chico stood by Shondra's door, dreading to knock but knowing he had to because he was on a mission for La and if he didn't come back with some kind of information soon, La was sure to have him do something worse that would definitely get him killed.

Shondra opened the door and let Chico in.

"Go to my room and take off your clothes and get ready for mama," She said directly. Chico sucked his teeth and walked to her room. He didn't enjoy fucking her anymore because she made it more of a duty than fun or leisure.

"What's wrong wit' you, boy?" she asked, removing the sundress she only wore to lounge around in while in the house.

"Ain't nothing. I'm not really in the mood. It's early," Chico responded, sitting on her bed changing the television channel with the remote.

"You not in the mood? Why? You was fucking wit' dat stupid young bitch in your building? Is that why?" she barked, snatching the remote out of his hands.

"Why you always buggin'? You got a man and you actin' like I'm him. You fuck with Junior, Shondra. That's your man. What me and you doing 'posed to be on the low but you trying to take it to another level and that ain't cool. He just caught us and you still acting like nothing happened." Chico's stress level was becoming evident.

"I'm not buggin', you li'l bitch. If you fucking me, you can't fuck near 'nother bitch out here, 'cause if you bring me something, you's gonna be a dead muhfucka. So that's not buggin', you fucking clown. And as far as Junior is concerned, mind your fucking business 'bout him. As

long as he don't catch you doing nothing, you don't have nothing to worry about," he replied harshly. Just then her telephone started ringing. She pressed the talk button on the cordless telephone.

"Hello?"

"Don't hang up. I need to ask you something important," the voice on the other end said. Shondra heard the familiar voice then turned to Chico and put her finger over her lips, signaling him to stay quiet. It was Junior.

"What you want?" Shondra walked into the living room to give herself privacy while she talked.

"I know you don't want to talk to me and trust me, I understand. I know I fucked up. But you ain't no saint in this shit no more either, Shondra. I know you fuckin' that li'l muhfucka and you playin' your fuckin' self!" The thought brought on rage in Junior and he soon forgot he was to be cordial in order to get the information he was seeking. "You ain't neva fuck wit' dudes 'round there, even before me and you got together, so how you gonna do that shit now? And don't tell me you not fuckin' him neither 'cause that bitch ass muhfucka couldn't even lie straight when he saw me! That's why I bloodied his shit!"

"First of all, muhfucka, I ain't fuckin' his bitch ass," she said screaming into the phone receiver. "Second, how could you bring that bitch 'round here again after I told you what she did. The bitch pulled a gun on me in the club, then the bitch pulled a razor when she came 'round here to fight me, and then *you* bring the bitch back around here and she pulled a fuckin' gun on me again and this time robbed me for my jewels!" Shondra was on fire as she thought of all the shit she went through with Muffin.

"I didn't know that. I only brung her with me 'cause I don't have nobody. I didn't expect you to be out there

anyway; *you* shouldn't have been out there. That's how I know you fuckin' that li'l muhfucka." Muffin never said anything to Junior about pulling a gun on Shondra.

"Please! And if I was fuckin' him, why the fuck would you care? You ain't fuckin' me no more! You got this shit twisted Junior; you really got me fucked up. I never stepped out on you the whole time we was together. I never stepped out on you no matter what the fuck people said. *You,* I knew you fucked some broads and got your dick sucked by them nasty-ass crack-smoking bitches, but you never brought that shit home to me, never. Now you actin' like you love this bitch more than me. You give that hoe more respect than you do me and you never did that before. You hurt me and you fucked me over. You the foul one in this!" Shondra's emotions were getting the best of her and she was talking loosely.

Chico listened to Shondra screaming on the phone like he wasn't in the room and couldn't hear her. He was paying close attention and soaking in everything being said. It would be his luck to hear something he could take back to La.

"She don't mean shit to me, Shondra," Junior said, lying through his teeth. "I told you why I'm playin' her close like that. I ain't tryin' to get locked up! You know I love you, baby. I don't love nobody else. That's my word!"

"Believe me, I tried to understand, but how much shit do you think I can take? I lost friendship with my best friend behind the bullshit you asked me to do and then you repay me by telling me you fuckin' that bitch to stay the fuck outta jail? Come on now, who the fuck I look like, Suzy Spongehead? You don't give a fuck about me and you don't give a fuck about our relationship, Junior."

Shondra was pacing the floor as she screamed on the phone.

Junior was speechless, he didn't have a comeback for what she said because she was right. He fucked everything up and it was all because of his feelings for Muffin. He tried to lie to himself in the beginning to believe he stayed close to Muffin so she wouldn't snitch on him but the truth was he had fallen in love with her. He was in love with both of them.

"I do give a fuck about you and our relationship, Shondra. I do. It's just that shit is so fucked up for me right now. That's what I'm tryin' to explain to you. You used to be in my corner through thick and thin, you used to hold me down no matter what; you used to be my Bonnie. I'm fucked up right now, Shondra. Ain't shit goin' right for me." Junior was almost pleading for understanding.

"What the fuck you talkin' 'bout? I was still there for you, Junior. I always been there for you. I never stopped: you did. You're fucked up because of you and the shit you done. You can't treat people like shit and expect good things to happen for you. I don't know if I can forgive you for fuckin' wit' that crazy bitch 'cause if things woulda worked out like she planned, I'd be dead."

"I know, Shondra, and I swear I'm sorry but I ain't really have no choice in doing some of the shit I do. It's part of the game," Junior confessed.

"But I'm not in the game…" Shondra started.

"Yes, you are. As long as I'm in the game you in it too," Junior informed her.

"No, Junior, you got it wrong. You in the game. I'm just a spectator," She explained.

"That's bullshit! You lived good with me, you enjoyed all the money and the jewels. I don't see you

givin' any of it back. I don't remember you ever tellin' me to get a job and give this shit up." He sucked his teeth. "I see how this shit works, when ole' boy down, muhfuckas forget shit, but when ole' boy get back on top, everybody ridin' his dick again!" Junior screamed into the phone receiver.

"I know you ain't talkin' 'bout me, muhfucka! I stuck by you. Don't forget I was there before you was makin' money. I was with you when you ain't had shit, so don't act like I got with you for some fake-ass fame and fortune!" Shondra yelled back into the phone.

"I'm talkin' 'bout every fuckin' body! You ain't no fuckin' different! Everybody flipped on me when I was gettin' money, dudes was tryin' to body me 'cause they jealous of what I got! I was scared and couldn't trust no fuckin' body I couldn't even trust my damn self, so when I started doin' shit to make sure I didn't wind up in Dante's Funeral Home or got railroaded by twelve muhfuckas in a box, everybody want to shit on me!" Junior eyes were tearing up.

"You know what, Junior? I used to think you really loved me, but now I can see that you don't give a fuck 'bout nobody but your fuckin' self. I'm not gonna sit here and let you talk that bullshit to me. Stay with that dumb bitch you fuckin'. But believe me: that bitch can't love you like I did. Fuck you…" Tears were forming in Shondra's eyes.

"Nah, Shondra, fuck you and that li'l faggot-ass bitch you fuckin'!" Junior's hurt came pouring out.

"Fuck you, Junior!"

"Fuck you…bitch!" Junior had never called Shondra that name before; it slipped.

"Bitch?" Shondra spoke in a calm voice because she wanted him to hear her clearly. "You call me a bitch? You call me out of my name after all the shit I've been through because of you and that slut? You know something, I felt guilty about what I told the police, but now I'm glad I did. You and that bitch gonna be cellmates real soon."

All Junior heard was a dial tone. He looked at the pay phone he was holding in his hand momentarily then slammed it down; he couldn't believe what he had just heard. His initial reason for calling her was to find out if the police knew anything about him and from her last statement, his question was answered. Now that he had his answer, he had to get away because it would be just a matter time before the police found him. But before leaving he was going to take care of all his unfinished business.

Junior & Muffin

"I think she snitched on me to the police," Junior was telling Muffin.

"What? See Junior, I told you that bitch never meant you no good. I know you ain't fuckin' with that hoe no more after this shit!" Muffin sat on the edge of her bed watching Junior pace back and forth across the room.

"I gotta get low. I ain't tryin' to get locked up. You down to go out of town?" Junior asked Muffin.

"I'll go anywhere with you, baby but why do we have to leave town. I mean, she don't know where I live and you been staying here with me," Muffin reasoned.

"I don't think she know where you live but I still need money, feel me? I can't hustle in Baptiste no more because I'll fuck around and get locked up if the noccos

catch me. Plus, I gotta take care of that muhfucka, La, for bangin' at me. And believe me, before it's all said and done, I'm gonna body him."

As Junior passed by the mirror on the dresser, he paused and looked at himself. The reflection showed a young man faced with issues he was ill-prepared to handle. Hustling had changed his life and his character into something he had no idea he would become. He was losing so much of who he really was because of the game he chose to be in. He once thought it would be easy to defy the odds and hustle without any problems. But his first taste of disloyalty forced him to make decisions he would never make otherwise. Hustling changed his whole life and he was losing so much in the process that he was becoming cold-hearted in order to cope.

"I'm gonna kill that muhfucka!" Junior screamed at the image in the mirror.

"Calm down, baby. I know you're mad but you gotta calm down," Muffin told him. Junior turned and looked at her. "I'm losin', Muff. Everybody flipping on me. I don't have nobody in my corner no more. The only person left is you and you might bail out on me too." He looked at her and lowered his head. Muffin got up from the bed and walked over to Junior and placed her hands around his waist and whispered into his ear. "I will never leave you Junior. I love you for real and I'm with you 'til the end."

"I hope you're serious, Muff, 'cause shit 'bout to get real serious now."

"It's about to get serious? It been serious, baby. Look at all the shit you've been through since I been dealing with you and I still ain't went nowhere. That should prove where my loyalty is," Muffin remarked.

"I know, baby. It's just that everything seems so fucked up right now. I know what I need to take care of but I ain't got no help now. It's like everybody just said fuck me," Junior walked over to the window and gazed outside.

"Junior, you don't need nobody. Fuck everybody that's shittin' on you right now. I'ma help you get back on your feet. I'll do whatever it takes 'cause I know you a hustler in your heart. Let's concentrate on what needs to be done first and let's do it, baby. Me and you. You said I was your Bonnie right?" she said, walking up behind him and hugging him around his waist.

"Yea, you my Bonnie…I hope." Junior turned around and stared into her eyes.

"I am, baby. Stop doubting me. I'm not gon' desert you like the rest of your fake-ass friends, family, and especially that stupid bitch. I'm gonna stand by my man," She said with heavy emphasis on the word "man." Junior looked at Muffin and felt a surge of trust he hadn't felt since going through all the drama the past year and half. Muffin made it clear through her actions and words that she had his back and wasn't going to leave his side, no matter what the circumstances. She was in for the long haul.

"I need to find another spot to hustle. I got a cousin in a small ass town in North Carolina that been asking me to bring some work down there to him for the longest. I wasn't wit' it before but now seems like a good time. And it's ideal because I can bubble down there and not worry about the police finding me. That town so small they would never think of looking for me there," Junior said to Muffin.

"You ever been there before, baby. I mean, you ever hustled there?" Muffin asked.

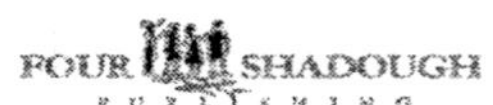

"Nah, I never hustled down there but I know it's money down there because I hit him wit' something a couple months back when he came here to visit. He called me two days later and been stressing me to come down there ever since. We was supposed to hook up but I never got around to it because of all the bullshit that started jumping off," Junior replied.

"Aight. I'm down with whatever you want to do, daddy. Just say the word," Muffin said, moving over to where he was sitting on the bed and rubbing his head.

"That's what I needed to hear. I got some things I need to take care of before I make plans on getting outta here. I gotta get my weight up first and then I gotta body that faggot-ass La before he catches me and puts out my lights. I thought he was dead the whole time and this muhfucka been sitting somewhere in the cut healing up so he could retaliate. The dumb shit is, I should be the one gunnin' at him 'cause he the one that tried to off me wit' your cuz. That muhfucka got a deathwish and I'ma seal his fate for him. He fuckin' wit' the right one." Junior stood up and looked up to the ceiling. "Plus I still gotta get the rest of my money from that young punk, Chico. He probably out there slingin' for La thinking I'm not gon' come back through there but I'ma creep on him one late night and get all mines…in blood if necessary. I already bloodied his shit so there's no mistake of my intentions once he sees me. Muff, once I get all this shit in order, we gon' bounce the fuck outta Brooklyn and turn it up in that country-ass town."

"So you gonna take care of that guy before we bounce outta here or you gonna wait?" Muffin asked.

Junior pondered for a minute before answering. "To be honest, Muff, I don't have the kind of money I used to have and my priority right now is to stack some bread before I go full blast with this dude. My money is mad low right now so I think I should get my weight up first and then handle my business with that snake-ass muhfucka."

"How much money you need to have before you go after him, baby?"

"It's not really a question of how much money, I just wanna have enough just in case. When you go to war you have to have enough money to hold you down so your full concentration can be on the matter at hand. I feel he still hustling in Baptiste and most likely got that li'l faggot-ass, Chico, working for him, so I plan on hitting him out there steady and bringing heat to his spot, which will slow down his money. It'll be hard for him to figure out a way to get money without getting pinched by the police while worrying about leaving himself wide open for a head shot through his Yankee fitted."

Junior cracked his knuckles. "That kind of pressure makes a dude move reckless and usually you can catch him off guard. That's what I plan on doing, baby. I plan on wearing him down first then sending him to see his homeboy, Kendu."

Junior looked at Muffin, feeling glad she was with him. He was starting to think more clearly and was focusing on things that needed to be handled more concretely. "Now I need to contact my peoples in the boondocks and see how it's clicking down there. Once I get the 411 on what's poppin' down there, I gotta make sure I get enough work to flood the town." Junior rubbed his forehead and his temple because the only person that could do that for him without him giving up any money was his cousin. He had a good relationship with their connect, Venezuelo, but to go to him like that would show

weakness and dependency. He didn't want to be turned down because his status in the game had changed. Craig was his only option to getting what he needed and regardless of promising himself not to fuck with him anymore because of what happened in the parking lot, he needed to humble himself to get the amount of work he needed to get back on his feet. It was now or never and time was not on his side.

Chapter 3
****K.B. & Gloria****

K.B. was sitting down in a lawyer's office signing the deed to the new barbershop he purchased from an old man who was getting out of the barber business. North Carolina was going to be his and Gloria's new residence and the purchasing of the barbershop would give them the financial stability they would need to live comfortably.

It had been a little over two months when they first arrived in Little Washington, North Carolina, for a rest stop. They were originally going to Atlantic Beach, North Carolina, and planned to stay in a hotel on the beach for a week to relax then drive down to Atlanta. On their way to Atlantic Beach, they followed Route 13 South to Route 17 South and had driven over seven hours before K.B. got tired and felt discomfort from the long ride. They approached a sign that read, "Washington City Limits" and he decided there was where they would stay for the night. An Econo Lodge hotel was to his left as he approached the traffic light that began the city limits of that town. He turned and looked at Gloria who was sleeping peacefully in the passenger seat of the car. He pulled into the left turn

lane and drove into the parking lot of the hotel and got a room for the night. He was so tired he didn't take their bags out of the car, instead he guided a sleepy Gloria to the room and placed her in the bed where she fell right back into a deep coma-like sleep. He snuggled up next to her and after about five minutes. He, too, was in a deep slumber calling the hogs.

They awoke famished the next morning, so they hurriedly washed their faces and ventured out to find somewhere to have some breakfast before getting back on the highway.

"Stop right there, baby" Gloria said, pointing to a Golden Corral restaurant.

K.B. pulled into the parking lot and they got out and went into the restaurant.

"This place looks cool. I hope they serve breakfast up in this joint," K.B. said, sitting down looking at the menu.

"They open, K.B., so they have to serve breakfast. It's only 11 a.m.," Gloria said to him.

A young Caucasian waitress approached them and asked them for their order in her most polite voice. Her country slang was so thick Gloria almost couldn't understand her when she placed her order. They received their order shortly after the waitress took it, gobbled it down quickly, and then left the restaurant.

"When is check-out time at the hotel?" Gloria asked K.B. as he pulled the rented 1992 Ford Taurus into the non-existent traffic on the highway.

"I think 12:00. Why?" he asked, heading in the direction of the hotel.

"Let's ride around for a minute and see what this town is about," she suggested.

"Aight, let's just make sure we know what check-out time is," he said, pulling into the hotel parking lot.

After confirming check out time was indeed 12:00, K.B. pulled the car back into traffic and traveled down the highway. As they drove, they passed small motels, gas stations, and restaurants then went around a slight curve where they could see a bridge off in the distance. They had only rode about ten minutes and passed three lights before seeing the bridge.

"I wonder if that bridge goes into another town?" K.B. inquired as they approached a stoplight.

"I hope not 'cause that means this town is about five minutes big," Gloria chuckled. K.B. pulled into a Phillips 66 gas station on the right to fill up the car.

"Excuse me, can you tell me where that bridge leads to?" K.B. asked the gas attendant while he paid for his gas.

"You not from 'round these parts, huh?" the attendant asked K.B., looking him up and down. "You's from up north, aintcha?"

"I'm from Brooklyn. I'm on my way to Atlantic Beach," K.B. responded.

"I kin tell you won't from 'round deez parts by your accent and the way you dress. That bridge o'er yonder will take you to Chocowinity," the attendant said, admiring K.B.'s apparel.

"Choco-what-aty?" K.B. missed something in the translation.

"Chocowinity; it's about eight miles 'cross that bridge. If you keep straight you'll be on the right road. Takes you to Morehead," The attendant explained.

"Aight, thanks man," K.B. said, holding his hand out for a shake.

"Don't mention it. Glad to be of some help," the attendant replied, shaking his hand.

"Is there anything in this town to see while I'm here?" K.B. turned and asked the attendant before leaving the gas station.

"Nope, you city folk prolly used to traffic and noise. You ain't gon' find none of dat down here in this town. There's a mall 'bout half a mile back from the direction you came. Or you can go to the waterfront downtown but ain't much to do there. Not like what you's probably used to up in the big city," the attendant spoke honestly.

"OK, well thanks anyway," K.B. said and walked out the door.

"Damn, Glo. Homeboy just told me there ain't shit to do in this town," K.B. said, sitting down in the driver's seat of the car.

"Well, let's ride around and see for ourselves. You never know what we might see. I ain't never been down south and I want to see how they live out here," Gloria said.

"Say no more, baby," K.B. replied. He pulled out of the gas station going in the opposite direction and made the first right and passed what looked like a storefront out of an old Andy Griffith sitcom. As he approached a stop sign on the corner he noticed another store but this one looked more like a house. There were a couple of guys standing in front and they all looked at the car as if they knew the occupants were from out of state. They continued driving until they came up on a stop sign, then made a left and passed what was the town's fire station. They continued straight, drove through a traffic light, and passed a cleaners on the left side of the street along with houses. They made a left by a big Catholic church and proceeded up the street.

There were no cars parked on the side of the streets; they were all parked up in driveways near the houses or in parking lots. They rode by a brick building that had silver letters on the front that read, "Washington Housing Authority."

Gloria looked at the small buildings that were connected to one another then said, "I know this ain't their projects?" K.B. wasn't sure because they looked like little houses, not projects.

"I'm not sure, but if these they projects, I wouldn't mind living there. They look way better than our projects," K.B. admitted, looking at the clean grounds and manicured lawns. K.B. turned left and drove slowly down the street pausing at every stop sign he came to then noticed a small barbershop on the left side of the street. He realized they passed by the shop already and had driven in a complete circle. The town was really small.

"Ay, Glo. I should go in there and get a haircut," he suggested.

"You trust these muhfuckas down here to cut your hair?" she asked.

"I don't think you can fuck up a edge up. You know what I'm saying?"

"OK, baby, it's your head," she said looking at his hair. He pulled the Taurus in front of the barbershop and parked.

"Come in there with me," he beckoned.

"I'm right behind you, baby" she complied, getting out of the car. They walked up the five steps to a porch and opened the glass door. A small bell rang when they stepped into the shop. There were three barber chairs but only one barber with graying hair on the sides, cutting an older gentleman's hair. When the tiny bell dinged, all eyes

shifted to K.B. and Gloria. There were three older gentlemen sitting on some chairs positioned against the wall as K.B. and Gloria passed by to sit in the unoccupied chairs next to them.

"Hey," one of the men said.

"How y'all doin' this mornin'?" another asked.

"Fine. Thank you," Gloria answered.

"I'm good," K.B. replied. "Who's next?" he asked the barber cutting hair.

"You are, youngin'." the barber replied, not looking up from the man's hair he was cutting.

Gloria picked up an old *Jet* magazine and started flipping through the pages as the men resumed a conversation they were having before the duo walked into the barbershop.

"My granddaughter don' went and got herself a good ol' boy from the country. I tells you, he be in those bacco fields every Saturday mownin' wit' his daddy," the old man sitting next to K.B. said.

"I should be so lucky. My grand courtin' sum young fool that mess with that dope. I declare, I can't understand these youngins today," the gray-haired old gentleman closest to the door said.

"Shucks, man. Dem young dope boys don' lost dere e'er lovin' mind foolin' with that mess. It don' destroyed half the town already," the man sitting next to K.B. stated.

"You ain't neva lie. I see dem fools that smoke that dope down there on da Block. It make dem crazy as a bear wit' his paw caught in a trap," the elder closest to the door replied.

"That's why I'm about to sell this here barbershop. I'm too old to be foolin' with dem crazy dope boys. They don't have no respect anymore, act like they own the world

cuz dey got demselves a li'l piece of change. Dey don't do nuthin' wit' da money but buy foolishness," the old barber said.

Hearing about the barber wanting to sell his barbershop gave K.B. a great idea. He could purchase the barbershop and take it off the old man's hand; he looked around and immediately thought about what he would do with it. When the barber was finished with his customer, he looked at K.B. and tapped the barber chair, cleaning it off with a white cloth.

"I want a fade but just a little off the top," K.B. said to the old barber as he sat in the chair.

"OK," the barber said, turning on his Oster clippers.

"How long you had this barber shop?" K.B. asked.

"Close to 40 years, had it since 1954. First black barbershop on this end of town," he said, beaming with pride.

"I overheard you saying you want to sell. Are you serious about selling?" K.B. asked him. The barber stop cutting K.B.'s hair and turned the chair around so he would be facing him.

"Where you from, boy? You come up in here and don't show no good manners by settin' right down and listen in on my conversation then got the nerve to ask me if I want to sell my barbershop?" the barber said.

"No, sir, I didn't mean no disrespect. I'm from Brooklyn and me and my girl," pointing to Gloria, "we down here on our way to Atlantic Beach. We stopped here in this town for the night and before we left she wanted to see the town. My name is Keith, Keith Burrows and I'm interested in taking this barber shop off your hands if you're serious about selling it," K.B. pitched sincerely.

"You want to buy my barbershop, huh New York boy? You want to buy my shop so you can turn it into a dope house. I know how you New York boys work. I seen ya come down in your fancy cars, with your fancy jewelry, and your slick talk. Well, sorry youngin', you won't turn this shop into no dope house," the barber said with conviction.

"Mister. You got it wrong. I don't sell no dope. I don't sell no kind of drugs. I'm looking for a new start in a new place and if I get the opportunity to run my own business, I'll stay here. I want to run a legit business, sir, straight up." K.B. was speaking with plenty emotion.

The owner of the shop looked at K.B. carefully. He was well-respected by other small business owners and his community because he had given many young people job opportunities that resulted in some of them being the first member in their family to go to college or even the first member of their family to open their own business. He had cut the hair of young children that he watched grow up to be strong, responsible men and it was something that gave him great pride.

Suddenly, the times changed and the young kids were losing respect for their elders. They didn't have the same morals and values that were once the cornerstone of the South. The new violent music that was being produced and the influx of that new drug corrupted the young minds in his beloved town and he was too old to fight the change. It was time to hang up his clippers and relax with his wife and live out his golden years in the modest home he built for them on his two acres of land. He looked at the young man who seemed so sincere and remembered a time when he was young with so much energy and dreams. He didn't want to take that away from the young man, so he

reluctantly agreed and prayed he was making the right decision.

"OK. Mr. Burrows, is it?" The old barber started. "I'm gon' give you a chance since you say you want to start o'er somewhere new. I'm not the trusting kind but I see something in you that speaks truth, so I'ma go out on a limb and ponder selling my business to you." He turned the clippers on and they made a low humming noise as he began cutting K.B.'s hair. "I own the building and the land this here shops sets on, you know, and I would hate to sell it and it winds up in the wrong hands." He looked at K.B. in the mirror. "I'm an ol' 'coon but I'm still sharp enough to spot a wolf. You wouldn't happen to be that wolf in sheep's clothing, now would you?"

K.B. looked at the old-timer and smiled. He was feeling him and understood the old barber's reasoning for keeping the integrity of his barbershop. K.B. knew exactly where he was coming from. He looked at Gloria and then replied to the barber, "Sir, I think I understand what you're saying and you can be sure ain't no wolf over here in sheep's clothing. That girl sitting over there is my reason for wanting this and I'm not going to let her down because she has been by my side throughout everything I've been through. I promise you I will not tarnish what you have built and will not disappoint you. I've seen a lot in my young life. I've been given a second chance and I'm not going to mess that up."

Gloria looked at K.B. and agreed to everything he was talking about, she was ready to begin their life in this new place, away from all the violence and broken friendships in Brooklyn.

Chapter 4
La

"That's all you got?" La scowled, counting the money Chico had just given him.

"It's been slow out here. The police always out here and they keep lockin' up the heads when they cop. It's been hotter than fish grease out here," Chico explained to La.

"I really don't give a fuck about the police being out here! I need my money for that pack. It's been two weeks and you babysittin' the shit," La growled.

"I'm tryin' to move this shit as fast as I can, La, but a lot of the heads scared to cop over here since the police fucking with everybody. One of the workers just got bagged with some work last night," Chico said, trying his best to explain the situation to La.

"Listen Chico, I don't give a fuck about what you sayin' right now. If it's hot out here then move somewhere else. You act like you can't think on your own! I gotta tell you everything? You sound like a li'l fuckin' kid complaining 'bout the police." La gritted his teeth.

"Aight, La, I'll move the shit to the other side of the projects. I'll tell one of the workers to stay out here and direct the fiends to the other side. I'll set up over there."

"Now was that hard? You wasted two fuckin' weeks bullshittin'. Now get my money, Chico, or there's gonna be problems the next time I gotta address this situation."

"Aight, man. But what you want me to do about that work the worker got busted with last night?" Chico asked.

"That's on you; I want all my money. You gotta eat that loss. If you think I'm gonna take a loss because you can't think for yourself then you got this shit twisted. Just have the rest of my money by the end of this week, no later. Next thing: did you find out from Shondra where that dirty muhfucka, Junior, staying or where he be at?" La asked.

"Nah, she ain't tell me nothing. I don't think she know where that bitch he fucking with stay," Chico stated.

"Is it that she ain't telling you shit because you ain't really asking her? Could that be it?" La lowered his eyes.

"That ain't it, La. To my knowledge, I don't think she spoke to him anymore since she told him she snitched on him and the bitch he fucking," Chico told him.

"You want me to believe that? You still fucking her right?" La asked, looking him directly in his eyes to see if he was going to lie.

"Yea, but it ain't like that. She trying to get serious now because I guess he not fucking with her like that no more," Chico said.

"Is that right? So you her man now?" La began laughing. "If that muhfucka find out you fucking her, he gonna kill ya punk ass."

Chico didn't find any humor in what La said because there was too much truth to what he said. Although he did like Shondra, Chico was turned off by the way she acted and treated him and it wasn't worth the risk of getting caught by Junior again. She was tyring hard to tie him down by taking up most of his free time so he wasn't able to fuck around with his old girlfriends the way he used to. She cockblocked every chance she got. He suspected her behavior changed because she and Junior weren't really together anymore. From the conversation he overheard in her house, it sounded like she was done with Junior.

All the drama he faced with Shondra and La was beginning to take its toll on him and he felt like he was going to self-destruct if he didn't get a handle on it quickly. He was tired of La with his threats and tired of Shondra with her demands. He wanted out of everything but felt he wasn't able, like he was stuck in a fucked-up movie. He never thought hustling would bring him so much bullshit he wasn't prepared to handle. His sole purpose for getting into the game was due to how people feared and respected all the hustlers in the neighborhood. Rock was a ghetto celebrity and was the center of attention when he was alive. He was intrigued by this and wanted to be down so bad but money wasn't his only motivating factor: it was more of the prestige of being a part of the whole scene. When he became Rock's right hand man, he was content with that position and felt safe, he felt he was untouchable. It was fun then but under La's reign, things were changing for him drastically, even the money came different. La paid him less than what Rock paid him and he was moving twice as much work. He was playing a grown man's game and was still a child himself. His situation

needed to change. At that moment he wished for something bad to happen to La so he could be rid of him. He thought it only because he wasn't capable to carry out the deed himself.

****Shondra****

Shondra sat by the telephone waiting for it to ring. She beeped Chico over an hour ago and he hadn't called back and she was growing impatient. She told him before he left her crib that morning she needed money to go shopping and get her hair and nails done. She was taking advantage of Chico unconsciously because she was used to getting money from Junior for everything she wanted. She knew Chico worked for La and made nowhere near the amount of money Junior did. Junior was a boss and Chico was just the help. But as long as he was fucking her, he was going to take care of certain things for her, no matter how much money he didn't have. Her desire for the finer things was bred into her from being the girlfriend of a boss.

Since she and Junior were on the outs she was beginning to realize he was more than just her man when they were together. He was her financier as well. The fact she never thought they would ever break up was the reason money was never an issue for her. Now, she was feeling the effects of being bankrupt. Her roots were getting nappy and her nails desperately needed a fill in.

Being the girlfriend of a hustler was not all it was cracked up to be because it robbed a woman of her independence by keeping her dependent on the man for everything. The woman usually found out the hard way what happens if he goes to jail or gets killed. At the funeral, she would find out she wasn't the only girlfriend and at the jail she will realize she isn't his only female visitor. In his death, she wouldn't have any say-so in the arrangements and once his body was in the earth, she'd be treated as if she was ride down for the deceased and not the loving couple she thought they were. And whatever money he had stashed in her house, oh, that belonged to the family. They will look for and take it, by any means necessary, even if they had to resort to strong-arm robbery. So-called friends will act like they want to help you out financially but she will soon realize there's a price attached to the money being given and if she's not ready to put out, the money train will end. This was just some of the things hustler girlfriends experienced. The life they lived in the beginning, when he was in full swing and getting that paper, shit is sweet. But if he ever falls, goes to jail, or dies…it's a wrap.

Because Shondra was bitter and angry about the shit she and Junior were going through, Chico was receiving the shitty end of the stick. He was the one that was around her so it was natural for her to take her frustration out on him without really thinking about his feelings. She was going to go embarrass him in front of his friends if she expected to keep him in his place. She had been around Junior long enough to know that most hustlers had delusions of grandeur, always acting like they had more than what they really did. They would buy flashy jewelry, expensive cars, and wear some of the finest apparel money could buy. They did this to achieve a phony status in the hood as being successful. Truth be told, all the jewelry, cars, and clothes amounted to nothing because they still lived in the hood and nine out of ten times were shacking up with a girl that was either on welfare or Section 8.

Shondra walked across the street to where Chico hustled. She was donning a blue handkerchief on her head to hide her hair, a pair of tight red Guess jeans with the matching sweatshirt, and a pair of blue Reebok Classics. She seriously needed to get her hair done and Chico was bullshitting, acting like he wasn't getting her pages. When she spotted him in the back of the building talking with one of his young bitches, she immediately got mad.

"Ay, boy!" she screamed out. Chico turned around and when he saw it was Shondra he saw the bullshit coming.

"What!" Chico yelled, frustration oozing out in his response.

"Who the fuck you screaming at, muhfucka!" Shondra yelled back to him, walking quickly to where he was standing.

"Damn, this bitch is getting on my fuckin' last nerve!" Chico quietly remarked to himself, as she got closer. The young girl he was talking to slid off, not wanting to get involved with anything with the older-skilled woman.

"Why the fuck you didn't call me back?" Shondra was in Chico's face. "I know you got my fuckin' beeps. You tryin' to duck out on me or something? I already told you not to fuckin' play with me, Chico." Shondra pointed her index finger in his face.

"What you want Shondra?" Chico breathed out heavily and his voice was nearly a whisper.

"You know what I want. I told you what I wanted this morning 'fore you left my fuckin' house. Stop fuckin' playin' with me, Chico," Shondra said in an aggravated tone.

"I ain't made no money, so you gonna have to hold up on that shit."

"I ain't gonna have to hold up on shit! You gonna give me what I need. You don't put me on hold, muhfucka; that's for them young slimy bitches you trying to fuck. I'm da Queen Bee, above everything and every bitch, so don't forget!" Shondra's neck was moving in a circular motion as she screamed at Chico.

"Why you talk like you a dude? Why you always riffing and shit like you got nuts or something?" Chico asked angrily.

"You tryin' to dis me? I will fuck your pussy-ass up! If I talk like a man it's because you act like a bitch!" Shondra hissed. When Shondra realized what happened, she was pulling herself up off the ground and tasting something thick and salty in her mouth.

"Oh, muhfucka! You want to hit a girl? You fucked up, Chico, that's my word. I'm telling my man and he gon' kill your faggot ass!" Shondra said while spitting blood onto the pavement.

Chico was at his boiling point with Shondra. She really pushed it when she called him a bitch. She had been disrespecting him and treating him like a chump so long that he almost forgot he was a young man. When he slapped her, it was an impulsive reaction and it felt good. He caught her totally off guard and when he saw her go down, he chuckled to himself.

"That muhfucka not fucking with your grimy ass no more. So stop frontin' bitch!" He yelled to her, walking to the other side of the projects.

What Chico said to Shondra hit home. She wiped the blood from her lips as she watched Chico walk down the block vindicated. She pushed him just a little too hard

and like any real man, he reacted. She began crying and couldn't stop, her body shook from her wails and she slowly slid back to the ground, hugging herself around the waist. She had finally come to grips with her tremendous lost. She and Junior were no more and Chico made it painfully clear.

***

"Yo, I'm tired of that bitch, kid," Chico was telling Smiley, one of the workers who worked on the other side of the projects. "She think 'cause she givin' me the pussy and 'cause she used to fuck with Junior that she can say what the fuck she want, like that shit holds weight. Yo, I just smacked the dog shit outta her 'fore I came over here."

"Yo, you wildin', son. That's Junior's girl. If she tell scrams you touched her he gonna come and put hands on you," the young hustler said, rolling up a blunt.

"That dude not fuckin' with her like that no more man. She washed up. And if she do tell him then I'm gonna have to handle my B.I. dat all." Chico said, poking his lips out and shaping his fingers like a gun.

"I heard that dude ain't the one to fuck with, Chico, so be careful. I heard he had a lot to do with some of the dead bodies found 'round here stinking some months back." Smiley cautioned, lighting his blunt.

"I ain't worried 'bout shit 'cause I can hold me down. Anyway, the bitch snitched on him so I don't think he gonna be coming through here like that anymore. He a smart dude. He ain't gon' risk getting knocked for her and her bullshit," Chico reasoned.

"She snitched on him? I thought she was a real thorough bitch. I guess when the wind blows, shit is bound

to hit you in your face." The young hustler replied, passing the blunt to Chico.

"Yo, you finished your pack?" Chico asked, changing the subject.

"Yea, and my count is right. You want it?" Smiley asked, digging in his pocket for the money then handing the neat stack to Chico.

"Now I gotta go check this crazy muhfucka and give him this money," Chico said, taking the money. "I'll come back with your next pack later on." Chico gave him dap and left.

Chico went back to his building and picked up the rest of the money he owed La then put it with the money he just received from Smiley. He looked at all the money he had and fantasized about it all being his. Many people believed money could solve all problems; it seemed to be the catalyst to success for anyone in the hood, no matter how they obtained it. It evoked fear, respect, jealousy, love and a whole wealth of other emotions one would think was not for sale. The bricks of money older hustlers pulled out and flashed around, the sleek expensive cars they purchased, and the expensive jewelry and clothing they wore were all signatures of making it in an environment where the weak could not survive. Chico was always fascinated by the power the hustlers exuded. But his virgin mind could not understand the ramifications of the game because it was clouded by the glitter and glamour that was seen externally when internally there was so much more below the surface. You had to be aware of and prepared for the consequences and repercussions, you had to be able lay claim to your territory and be willing to fight, kill, and even die to protect it. The real truth was that no hustler controlled the Block and no hustler owned any real estate

in the hood. They were all playing street politics or acting out a character from their favorite gangster movie and everyone was playing on borrowed time. Yea, that's the game; you can try to make it your reality but when the time comes, game over.

When Chico emerged from his building, he noticed a dark blue undercover Impala pulled up beside him and he heard the siren before he even saw the vehicle next to him.

"Woop, Woop." The siren was meant to get his attention.

"Ah, shit. What the fuck these muhfuckas want?" Chico said, stopping in his tracks. Taylor got out first from the passenger side of the vehicle.

"Ay, come over here," Taylor called out to Chico.

"Man, what you want. I ain't doin' nothing," Chico said, walking over to the shabbily dressed detective.

"Did I say you did anything? Now that makes me believe you may have done something," Taylor said, eyeing Chico's pockets.

"What you want?" Chico asked when he was about five feet from the detective.

"Your story, that's what I want. You have one to tell me?" Taylor said, turning around briefly to see if his partner had exited the vehicle.

"I don't have no story to tell. How 'bout you tell me one," Chico said sarcastically.

"OK." Taylor looked at Burke then continued: "Me and my partner are still investigating the murder of your friend and we haven't heard anything from you since we last spoke. That's not good and we still haven't gotten any leads; however, we may have a breakthrough." Taylor paused and looked in Chico's eyes to see if he was listening then went on. "Well, the breakthrough is, we

found the murder weapon but that's not it. Here's where the story gets interesting: we know who it belongs to."
Taylor looked at Burke then back to Chico, who seemed not to understand what was happening.

"Want to know who the suspect is?" Taylor edged.

"Sure," Chico said. Taylor laughed low in his throat, "You should want to know. I mean, I would too if I were in your position." Chico got what Taylor was implying and began to fear the worst.

"Yo, don't try and pin shit on me 'cause I ain't kill nobody," Chico confessed.
Taylor looked to his partner and shrugged his shoulders. "Did I say you killed anyone? I don't remember implicating you as a suspect, but since you're so quick to be on the offensive I think my partner and I may have to rethink this thing. What you think, Burke?" Taylor asked, looking to his partner for a response.

"I think you may be right, partner. From my experience, if you pull a dog's tail, he'll bark. And if you pull a cat's tail, she'll meow. And when you pull a criminal's tail they'll say, 'I ain't kill nobody," Burke chuckled to himself.

"Look man, I ain't do shit. Y'all tryin' to set me up. Why y'all always fuckin' wit' muhfuckas for nothin'? Ain't there some real crime happenin' somewhere else? Don't y'all have anything else to do besides fuckin' with dudes in the hood?" Chico backed away from the detectives.

Taylor looked at his partner who just nodded his head. Taylor grabbed Chico by his collar before he could get too far and threw him on the trunk of the car and handcuffed him.

"See what running off with the mouth can get you, youngster?" Taylor said, dragging him to the back door of the car.

"What the fuck you lockin' me up for?" Chico managed to say once he caught his breath after being thrown onto the trunk of the Impala.

"What do we have here?" Taylor said, pulling a wad of money from Chico's front pocket. "Wait, don't tell me, this is money to pay a bill or you're just holding it for someone but it ain't yours, right?"

"It ain't my money for real," Chico said in between breaths.

"OK, then you shouldn't have it," Taylor said, putting the confiscated money in his pocket then shoving Chico into the backseat of the Impala.

"You lockin' me up for havin' money on me that's not mine?" Chico asked, slumping down in the back seat of the car. Taylor slipped into the passenger side of the vehicle then turned to Chico. "No. You're getting arrested because you're a suspect in two murders."

"Man, I ain't kill nobody in my whole life. Look, y'all got the wrong guy. I swear I ain't never hurt nobody." Chico played right into Taylor's plan.

"I'm not sure I can take your word on that," Taylor said, pulling out a gun in a sealed plastic Ziploc bag, "This weapon here has your prints all over it."

"Yo, that's bullshit!" Chico whined, inspecting the gun from the backseat. "That ain't my gun. I don't even own a gun. That's somebody else's gun. That shit ain't mine."

"Well, if it isn't yours, whose is it?" Taylor asked.

"I don't know but I know it ain't mine," Chico reinforced.

"Well, as far as we know, it's yours and that's the story we're sticking to unless you can prove otherwise," Taylor smirked, looking over to his partner. Chico didn't know if the detectives were serious. All he knew was they were accusing him of something he definitely didn't do and he didn't want to end up in jail for murder.

"Look man, I swear I didn't do anything. I swear y'all have the wrong person," Chico pleaded. Taylor looked over to Burke, winked his eye, then looked at a frazzled Chico in the backseat.

"Do you have any idea whose gun this is then? A couple of weeks ago we were dispatched to where you guys sell your drugs because of gunshots in the area. This is one of the weapons we found out there that day. There have been a lot of unsolved murders in this area. I'm going to be honest with you: my superiors want these cases solved. I don't want to arrest the wrong person but I have to go with the evidence I currently have…unless I get some new evidence or leads in the case." Taylor was eyeing Chico carefully reading his facial expressions. "Now, if you say you aren't the one that had anything to do with the murders then maybe you have some information that can help me get the right person and clear your name."

"Aight. I'm not sure if that's the same gun but this dude hit me with a gun that looks just like the one you got in that bag," Chico revealed. Taylor looked at Chico and noticed the bruise on his face, leading him to believe there was some truth to his statement.

"What's his name?" Taylor asked hungrily, waiting for the name he expected to hear.

"Junior. His name is Junior," Chico snitched.

"Junior? So why did he hit you with the gun?" Taylor asked.

"Over a bitch. He think I'm fuckin' wit' his girl," Chico said, squirming in his seat.

"Well…Chico. It is Chico right?" Burked asked. "That's really just your word against his. The only way we would know is if we brought him in for questioning. Do you know where he is or where he hangs out?"

"Nah, I don't know where he lives. I don't know him like that," Chico responded.

Chico could tell the detectives were trying to have him do the same thing La was asking him to do in finding out Junior's whereabouts.

"OK, this is what I'm gonna do Chico," Taylor started. "I'm going to hold up on this investigation until you're able to get me the information I need to question this Junior. Take this number and, this time, use it. As soon as you find out where he is, give us a call. Even if you see him in the area, give me a call and I'll try and get him on the streets if I can't get him at a secured location. Do you understand?" Taylor asked, dropping the card on his lap.

"Yea, I understand," Chico replied.

Burke pulled up to the place where they picked Chico up and Taylor got out. He went to the back and pulled Chico out then uncuffed him.

"You have that card I gave you with my number on it?" Taylor asked.

"Yea, I got it," Chico replied.

"OK, you have two weeks to give me a call with some information. If not, I'll come back looking for you. And believe me, I won't be as generous as I was today," Taylor said, grabbing the handle of the cruiser.

"Can you give me back the money you took from me?" Chico asked Taylor. He opened the passenger side

door. "What money?" he said. The Impala pulled off and left Chico standing in the middle of the block.

"Gotta give it to you, partner, you worked that young boy like a true professional," Burke said to Taylor.

"I told you we're gonna solve some of those murders and get the lieu off our back. I'm tired of watching these drug dealers benefit off the backs of the taxpayers and get away with murder while they do it," Taylor confided to his partner.

"I agree. And hopefully we'll get this Junior character back in our clutches after your informant calls you. Then we'll be able to close at least one of the many murder cases we have open," Burke said.

"Yea, I just hope he does it within the timeframe I slotted for him. If not, we're going to have to find another way to get this guy. Hey, pull over there to the restaurant; I'm famished," Taylor directed.

"I'm tapped out this week, partner" Burke said, pulling inside the restaurant parking lot.

"That's OK, it's on me. I just came into some money," Taylor laughed, pulling the money he took from Chico out his pockets. He exited the vehicle and headed to the entrance of the restaurant. "Lunch is on Chico today."

****La****

The department store clerk was writing her number down on a $100 bill and passing it to the young black customer paying cash for his Pioneer audio entertainment system.

"This way you know I'll call you," La said to the light-skinned clerk.

"I don't know…that might be the last one you have, so you might spend it before you call me," she smiled seductively.

"Don't worry, hun," La began, pulling out a stack of money and peeling through it so she could see all the hundred dollar bills, "I have so many I won't have to spend this one for years. I'm gonna give you a call tonight. What time do you get off?"

"I get off at 6," she replied.

"You feel like hanging out tonight?" he asked, leaning in closer to her.

"Sure, why not? Where you tryin' to go?" she asked, smiling ear to ear.

"Look, I'ma keep it real wit' you. If you want to go out and eat we can do that, but I don't want the night to end at a restaurant, you feel me?" La's eyes were piercing and searching her soul for realness.

"Well, we'll have to see how the night goes before I swear to that," she replied while blushing.

"That's fair. I'm gonna give you a call about 7, 7:30 and I'll pick you up and we'll go to Red Lobster or sumthin'," La said, turning around and walking away not waiting to hear her reply.

"Damn, he look good," she said to herself, watching him disappear in the sea of customers in the store.

La was always confident and had always been a ladies man before getting shot. But he projected a new air of confidence that made him more dominant whenever he talked to anyone. He survived the attempt on his life and beat the odds by recovering from his wounds completely. Then he accomplished what he set out to do, from the very beginning, which was to take over the drug trade in Baptiste alone with no help. In the process of the takeover,

a ruthless murderer surfaced inside, changing him forever. He was able to kill someone he had known for years without showing any remorse whatsoever. This newfound power was what he wanted early on and he finally had it. He had no intentions of losing it—not like the rest who were on top for a while then fell off. Not La. His plans were to stay at the top. The way to ensure that was to make sure he got rid of Junior. Once that was carried out, he would be able to fall back and concentrate on building a team of workers that would fear him as if he were God himself.

When La pulled up in front of his building, he didn't see any workers or traffic so he went to the other side of Baptiste to see if Chico was around. He needed to pick up his money. When he pulled up in front of one of the buildings he saw one of the workers and got out of the car.

"What's up, Smiley? What's your count?" He asked the young worker.

"I already hit Chico with it a coupla hours ago," Smiley replied, waving a customer to the back of the building.

"OK, cool. Everything aight out here?" La asked, following him through the building to observe how he served his customer.

"E'erything good out here," Smiley replied, placing two small capsules on the ground, then pocketing the money the customer handed to him.

"Ain't nobody out here watching your back?" La asked, looking around for another worker.

"Nah, ain't no need for two workers out here right now. The late night rush is when I need somebody to

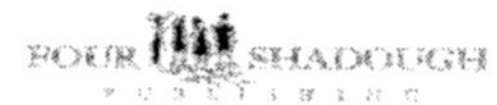

watch me," he explained to La as they walked back to the front of the building.

"OK, that's peace. As long as you aight with that, I'm good," La said, slapping him five and walking back to his car. On his way back to the other side of the projects, he spotted Chico walking up Montrose Avenue.

"Ay, yo!" La yelled out the window, slowing the car down. When Chico heard the all-too-familiar voice, his heartbeat raced and he slowly turned around. La beckoned him to the vehicle and Chico moved toward the car like a slug.

"What's up, La?" Chico said in a nervous tone, stuffing both hands in his pockets.

"Ain't nuthin', boy. I just bagged me a cutie and I'ma slay that ass later on," La bragged. "You picked up from Smiley?"

Chico hadn't figured out what he was going to tell La. He knew that if he spoke out of fear, La wouldn't believe him. "Nah, I ain't picked up from him yet, he said it was slow. I'll go pick up when he 'bout to end his shift," Chico said, lying through his teeth.

La looked at Chico and wondered who was lying to him. He tried to read Chico's eyes but they were steady and sure. He was about to tell him he just left Smiley but changed his mind.

"He said it's slow out there?" He asked Chico, his head tilted to one side.

"Yea, I told you it's been hot out here with all that shooting that happened. The heat be out on the regular," Chico said.

"But didn't I tell you to change up the rotation or change the spot until shit cools down? You can't let them

muhfuckas stop us from eating, B," La said, paying attention to how Chico was rocking back and forth.

Chico continued spinning his tale. "I know and I told Smiley to move the spot to the bodega on Broadway. He said it was hard to let all the heads know on short notice."

"That's what he told you?" La asked him.

"Yea."

"Aight, get in the car," La said. Chico walked over to the passenger side of the Maxima and got in when he heard the clicking of the automatic door locks. La didn't say anything when Chico entered the car, he just sped off. They pulled up and parked across the street from where Smiley was working and got out of the car.

Chico suddenly felt nauseous. He felt La was going to ask Smiley where the money was. Once Smiley revealed to La he had given him the money, all hell would break loose.

"Come on!" La said to Chico. "I'ma show you why muhfuckas 'posed to pay attention and follow what's told to them." La walked toward the building and spotted Smiley in the lobby.

"Yo, Smiley, follow me upstairs," La said, pushing the button for the elevator.

Smiley slapped Chico and La five, not sensing any danger. When the elevator arrived La opened the door and everyone got on. La pressed the sixth floor button and the elevator glided up to the last floor of the building. He pushed opened the elevator door when it stopped, walked straight to the exit, then headed up to the roof. Chico and Smiley were behind him but Chico's legs were weak beneath his 120-pound frame. La opened the roof door and

stepped into the evening air. Chico paused at the roof door, took a deep breath, then walked onto the roof with La.

"You know what I hate?" La turned around, eyeing both young men. No one answered; they just looked at La as if he were President Bush about to give a State of the Union address.

"You know what I'm not going to tolerate? I'm not going to tolerate any bullshit from anybody that works for me. No snitching, no lying, no disloyalty, nothing! The first time I think one of my workers is doing something dirty behind my back I'm going to eliminate them…period!" La roared.

Smiley became nervous, his mind racing, trying to find out if he violated in any way, but he couldn't think of anything. Chico looked at La and feared the worst was about to happen.

La turned his back to both men and walked to the edge of the roof, the gravel beneath his feet sounding like shaking maracas. He looked over the edge and spoke to no one in particular when he said, "It's a long way down when you're up so high." Then he turned to Smiley and Chico and continued. "Right now, I'm on the top." He spread his arms out and turned in a full circle. "Standing here, I can go no higher but one thing is for sure…I'm not going to fall from where I stand right now because my feet is on solid ground," he said as he stomped his feet. "And I'm not going to allow another muhfucka to make me fall by lying to me or trying to steal from my plate!"

"Yo, La, I ain't neva do you dirty. I always keep it official with you," Smiley spoke up.

"I know you do, that's why you here, ain't that right…Chico." La directed his glare to Chico, pulling out a massive magnum from his waistline. Chico wanted to turn

and run away and never come back but he couldn't move; he was immobilized by fear. He had a lump in his throat and his palms were clammy.

"Yo, Smiley, where is my money?" La turned to face Smiley.

"Huh?" Smiley asked puzzled.

"You need me to repeat myself? I said where the fuck is my money!" La cut his eye to Chico. Smiley looked at La then at Chico and his young mind couldn't fathom what was being asked of him. He had given Chico the money hours ago and just told La that, no less than half an hour ago.

"I gave—" Before Smiley could finish his sentence, he saw a flash of light and heard a boom that sounded like thunder in a rainstorm and he collapsed onto the graveled rooftop like a felled tree.

La walked over to the fallen youth and stood over him pressing the steel barrel hard against his forehead, while he held his thigh screaming at the top of his lungs.

"Shut the fuck up! I should kill your fuckin' ass for trying to steal from me, muhfucka!" La hissed, cocking the hammer back on the magnum. Smiley was unable to answer from the mixture of fear and pain he was experiencing. He couldn't believe La shot him over something he didn't do.

Then La turned to Chico with a wicked look in his eye. "Should I finish him Chico?" Chico was stiff and couldn't answer. The events happened so quickly Chico was unsure if what he was witnessing was real.

"Chico! Should I kill this lyin' muhfucka!" La barked, pressing the barrel harder against Smiley's forehead.

"N-n-nah, La. Don't kill him, man" Chico stammered, backing away toward the roof door.

"Why the fuck not? He fuckin' wit' my money. Why shouldn't I kill him?" La questioned devilishly, stepping on the leg of a squirming Smiley.

"I don't know, La. Just don't kill him, man. Please." Chico begged.

La knelt down and whispered in Smiley's ear. "I'm glad Chico told me about your stealing ass but you're getting a pass today. You're one lucky bastard. You better thank him for saving your life!"

La walked over to Chico who was visibly shaken with tears in his eyes, then told him, "Come on 'fore the police come."

As they ran down the stairs Chico asked, "We just gonna leave him up there like that?" La stopped on the second floor landing and turned to Chico. "What you suggest I do, call 911 or take him to the hospital? What the fuck, you want to go back up there and tend to his wounds? You a fuckin' doctor now?"

La turned back around and descended the stairs into the lobby and peeked out the entrance door, then put his head down and quickly walked to his car and got in. When Chico got in on the passenger side, La pulled off slowly and headed for the other side of the projects.

Chico's conscience was getting the best of him. He felt sick to his stomach about Smiley getting shot for something he was guilty of. But after seeing what La did to him, he preferred that Smiley rather than him received La's wrath of fury.

"See what happens if you steal or lie to me, Chico?" La looked at him in the eyes.

"Yea, man; I see," Chico said, his body trembling in fear.

La originally thought that once he pulled up in front of the building Chico would come clean but when he didn't, La changed plans and decided to send a strong message instead. His logic didn't make sense but the result was powerful. He wouldn't have to worry about Chico coming up short or stealing a dime from him, no matter what. He was confident his operation was going to run smoothly from this point on. He glanced over at Chico and could clearly see the blanket of fear on his face. There was no denying La had turned into a dangerous man and he liked the feeling of power along with the steady flow of money. Although he had gotten shot in his first takeover attempt, he had no regrets. In his twisted mind he felt that was the price to pay to be where he was now.

The car pulled up in front of Chico's building and Chico hurriedly grabbed the door handle to exit.

"Hold on, Soldier," La said, grabbing his arm firmly.

Chico stopped and looked at La with wide eyes.

"How you plan to pay for that money you fucked up?" La asked.

"Huh?" Chico began fearing the worst.

"You didn't hear me? Let me explain this shit to you one more time so you won't get this shit twisted." La was staring at Chico like a madman. "Whenever I put something in your hands, it's yours soon as you take it. You are solely responsible for it from that point, understand me?" Chico nodded.

"Now tell me how you gonna pay me my money." La tilted his head to left.

"I don't have no money La."

"That's sounds personal, B. See, I don't care where you get it from I just want it. You do understand me don't you?" La hunched his shoulders and peered into Chico's eyes like he was trying to look through him. Chico nodded his head again.

"Now, for the last time, tell me how you're going to pay me." La started reaching for his magnum slowly.

Chico thought for a second. "I can pay you off the next two packs you give me. I won't take any PC off it. I'll give you everything."

"How you plan on doing that? You don't work the buildings," La said, raising an eyebrow.

"I know, but I'll sling the next two packs myself," Chico told him.

"Aight, sounds like a plan. Just make sure you have everything. No shorts!" La patted the gun in his waist.

"I hear you, La. It'll all be there," Chico said while keeping an eye on La's hand movements.

La's pager went off. He unclipped it from his pocket and looked at the screen but didn't readily recognize the number.

"Oh shit, this probably that shorty I met earlier. Aight, get the fuck outta my whip so I can go get clean and pick up this broad," he told Chico, waving him off.

Chapter 5
K.B. & Gloria

"You reckon the guy that bought the shop gon' really cut hair?" A strapping young man asked his friend standing in front of a store.

"Look here, mane, if dat dere guy is from New Yawk, he gon' be slangin' dope outta dere fo' sho'," his equally muscular friend replied.

The blue awning was positioned over the small brick building with the words, "New York Kutz" emblazoned in white lettering. Gloria and K.B. were inside tidying up before the grand opening. K.B. wanted to give the barber shop a New York feel so he invested heavily in having the floor tiles spell out the word "Brooklyn" as you entered into the shop. He had mirrors cut out in the shape of the borough of Brooklyn in front of each barber chair and on each headrest, embroidered were the letters "NYK." The customer waiting chairs were plush leather and very comfortable. Beside each chair was a small table that had the newest hip-hop magazines—*The Source*, *Word UP*, and *XXL*— along with *Jet*, *Essence*, and other black-themed magazines, neatly placed on them. K.B. hired three

licensed barbers and had one of the chairs dedicated to a female who specialized in braids and weaves. He was going to make sure his business would be completely legitimate because he became concerned when he found out it was located in a high-traffic drug area.

In the South, people were normally friendly and pleasant but K.B. was not used to it being from the city and all. Two country boys approached him while he was cleaning the outside of the shop, getting it ready for business.

"How ya doin'?" one of the guys inquired as K.B. emptied out a bucket into a garbage can in front of the shop. K.B. turned around, not recognizing the guys, and shifted his weight from one foot to the other.

"I'm good, what's up?" K.B. answered, peering at both boys, his Brooklyn instincts kicking in.

"Dis here Old Man Washington barbershop. You kin to him?" the other stocky country boy asked, looking K.B. up and down.

"Am I what to him?" K.B. asked defensively.

"Kin. You's his family? I'm askin' 'cause I sees you cleaning up and changin' how thangs lookin' in dar," the stocky one continued, in his thick country tongue.

"Oh, nah, man, he ain't my fam like that. I bought this shop. It's mine now," K.B. clarified.

"Old man Washington sold his barbershop? I knew that ole' coon was gon' get off da Block soon 'nuff," the stocky guy said to his friend, who was looking inside the shop at K.B.'s girlfriend's fat ass.

"Mmm hmmm. I knew he was gon' leave, too," the friend replied, still looking at Gloria, who was bent over sweeping something into a dustpan. "Hey, cuzzin, you from up North aintcha? I can tell by your accent."

"I'm from Brooklyn," K.B. answered, turning around to continue cleaning up the front of the shop.

"So you gon' be runnin' da barbershop?" The friend asked. Annoyed, K.B. looked at the two young men then answered. "Yea, I'm the owner. You want a haircut? The Grand Opening is today."

"Heh, Heh. Sure, mane, I get a cut once a week. Awright, guess we'll let you gon' back to settin' up yur shop. I'll let the boys 'round here know. Holla atcha soon," the stocky country boy said, then he and his comrade turned and walked off.

K.B. continued getting the shop ready but watched the boys from the corner of his eyes. He was almost certain they were selling drugs and felt they would be his customers in the long run along with the other dealers on the Block. He went back into the barbershop and admired how he transformed the old shop into something more modern and inviting with a taste of home to give him a constant reminder of where he was from.

Gloria was putting streamers and balloons all around the inside of the shop in preparation for the Grand Opening. K.B. ordered five buckets of chicken, cole slaw, potato salad, and biscuits from KFC for the patrons. He and Gloria were so excited and he felt all business as he walked into his back office and sat down behind his desk in his leather swivel chair. This was a smart move for him and he was going to make it work. He was going to steer clear of any bullshit that arose and was going to become a well-respected business owner like the old man that gave him his golden opportunity.

Gloria walked into his office smiling lovingly. "Baby, I'm so excited. You made it look so nice in here. I

can't wait 'til the barbers and hairdresser get here so we can open it. I'm so proud of you K.B.," she said sincerely.

K.B. got up from behind the desk and walked over to where Gloria was standing and wrapped his arms around her waist and kissed her slowly. Then he stepped back and looked at her at arm's length. "None of this could have been possible without you, baby. We did this together. This is our business, this our new start, our new beginning. I love you, Glo'. You are the reason for this. You made this possible and I'm glad you stuck with me through it all."

Gloria eyes welled up. "I'm just glad we're able to be standing here together, baby we've been through so much the past year that I'm just thankful to be here with you by my side. I will go through it all again if I know I would have you in the end."

A small chime alerted them that someone entered the shop and they both walked out the office to see who it was.

"Hey there." A young man greeted them as he walked into the shop.

"How you doin'?" K.B. asked, approaching with his right hand outstretched for a handshake.

"I'm Jerome Wilkins, I'm one of the new barbers," he said, shaking K.B.'s hand.

"No doubt. My bad. I shoulda recognized you with your barber coat on," K.B. replied. "Since you the first one to arrive you can pick your chair."

Jerome looked around, impressed with the layout of the shop. "You got it lookin' right nice in here. Never seen a shop fancied up like this," he said, gazing around the entire shop. "You sure gave it a comfortable feelin', I can tell you that much." Jerome picked the first chair and sat down. "Yea, I'm a like this one right here."

K.B. introduced Jerome to Gloria and they chatted awhile before the second and third barber walked in. William Gorham and Terrence Hodges, respectively, introduced themselves to K.B., Gloria, and Jerome. K.B. was surprised each barber knew one another, then remembered how small the town really was. Things looked like they were going to work out smoothly with the business and K.B. couldn't be happier. As everyone talked amongst themselves, the door chimed once again and in stepped a young, fair-skinned girl. Her body was goddess-like: she had full breasts that protruded from the red form-fitting sweater she was wearing, her small waist exploded by her hips, which were perfectly round and made the jeans she wore look painted on, and her thighs complemented her shape by staying in proportion with her hips. She had deep-set dimples in both cheeks and her eyes were round and soft. Her hair was styled in a Chinese bob and her skin was flawless with not a scratch to be found. K.B.'s eyes were glued to the beautiful girl whose youth shown through her demeanor. She was smiling, almost giggling at K.B., who caught himself with his mouth wide open.

"Hi, I'm Patricia Newkirk, the hairdresser," she said to no one in particular. It was more like she was announcing her presence.

"Hi, Patricia. My name is K.B. and I'm the owner," K.B. said, way too lovingly for Gloria.

"Hi, Patricia. My name is Gloria and I'm the co-owner and fiancée of the owner." Gloria didn't see the look on K.B.'s face when Patricia first walked in but there was no denying her youth, beauty, and firmness. Her claws immediately came out and she was going to make it clear from the onset that K.B. would be off limits.

K.B. caught himself but it was too late because of Gloria's statement. The girl standing in front of him was a fine specimen of a woman, not taking anything away from Gloria but she had a certain energy surrounding her that made K.B. become instantly weak. His mind and emotions were mincemeat and Gloria suddenly felt a twinge of jealousy and unsuredness with the new addition to the business.

Chapter 6
Shondra & Junior

Shondra tried dialing the number again and put in her phone number for the tenth time. The reality of what Chico told her prompted her to find out if there was any salvaging of her damaged relationship with Junior's damaged relationship. She was feeling bouts of insecurity because she never believed they would ever break up for good. It had been months since she'd spoken to or seen him and he hadn't made any attempts to contact her. She was beginning to believe he was over her and was in the arms of, Muffin. Before she jumped to conclusions, she needed to know for sure, she needed to see him once more and talk with him to see if that's what he really wanted.

She sat by the phone waiting for him to return her call although she had a strong feeling he wouldn't. He always told her the only way he would leave her for good was if she snitched on him or set him up. In her defense, she didn't mean to tell the detectives on him but at the time she was so upset and hurt that it didn't matter at the time. She would have never done anything like that but all the shit she been through with Muffin was too much to bear.

As much as she tried to understand him and what he tried to make her believe about his relationship with Muffin, it was a bunch of bullshit to her. Shondra knew he gave the bitch too much power. He was showing Muffin more respect as if Muffin was his girl and she was the mistress. It wasn't fair, she thought. He wanted her to play the back seat in their relationship to that bitch. And the ultimate violation was that he still fucked with Muffin after she threatened Shondra's life, not once, but two times.

Tears rolled down her face as she tried to make sense out of her tumultuous life with Junior. Her emotions were getting the better of her so she went outside to get some air. It was difficult for her to accept the end of their relationship, even though Junior was the one that was wrong. After being slapped to the ground by Chico, she realized she needed to find out if there was a chance left between her and Junior; at the very least she needed closure.

She had no idea where he was, what he was doing, or how he was getting along. Despite what he had done, she was still in love with him because they had a history together. They shared so much and for it to be over the way it was happening was literally tearing her apart. She had lost as much as Junior claimed but her losses were also more of a personal nature. She lost her best friend because of a decision she made for him. To lose him too just wasn't fair to her. It was like losing him was her punishment for her disloyalty and betrayal of her friend, Gloria.

She walked out of her building, unsure of where she was going. But then she started walking toward Tompkins Projects in hopes of running into Junior. As she walked up Myrtle Avenue, she noticed Junior's cousin Craig standing

in front of a bodega talking to a pretty young Puerto Rican girl with blonde streaks in her hair.

"Hey, Craig," she said, approaching him from behind.

"Oh shit. What's up, Shondra?" he replied, greeting her with a warm hug.

"Nothing much. How you been?" she asked, inspecting the girl he was talking to.

"I'm good," he said, hungrily eyeing the Spanish girl he was talking with.

"Um, can I talk to you real quick…in private?" she asked.

"Um, yea, sure," he said, whispering something into the young chica's ear. "What's up, what's on your mind?"

"I'm sorry, Craig. I didn't mean to stop you from what you were doing, but I'm looking for Junior. I haven't seen or heard from him in about a month," she stated honestly.

"Oh. Well, me and him on the outs right now. I ain't really fucking with him like that," Craig said, watching a police cruiser driving slowly pass them.

Shondra was shocked to hear that. She thought for sure when she saw Craig she would at least find out if Junior was all right.

"What happened? I mean, I know it's none of my business, but it's funny to hear you say you not fuckin' with him no more like that and you his family."

"Well, not fo' nothin', he was actin' stupid over something he was warned about before he got in the game and I was tired of hearing him trying to blame other people instead of standing for what he know. Ya feel me? That's my fam and all but he needed to wake up and stop cryin' over all the shit he been through. He chose to do this shit.

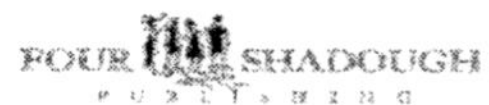

Nobody put a gun to his head and made him do it. He responsible for the choices he made, nobody else," Craig explained.

"He told me he was going through a lot and seeing that even y'all had problems, I really believe him. But at the same time, he shitted on me with some bitch he fuckin'." Shondra's tone of voice changed. "The bitch tried to off me, Craig, and this muhfucka still fuckin' with her. The worst part is, it didn't just happen once, it happened twice. I told him what she did and he steadily fuckin' with her like he don't give a fuck about me or my feelings." Shondra had so many confused emotions consuming her that she needed to let it out and Craig was going to be her vessel.

"I was there for him, Craig. I been there before all this shit started with him getting money and everything. I don't understand why he just flipped on me like that for that bitch, I just can't figure it out."

"Let's go over by my car so we can talk more in private," Craig said, guiding her across the street to the parking lot off of the main street to avoid eavesdropping passersby. She followed him to his Benz and allowed her tears to flow freely once away from the bodega.

"Know what I think, Shondra? And this is off the record…" Craig began as he sat on the hood of his Benz. "My cousin had this false sense of safety in what he was doing; he didn't anticipate all that came with him getting this money. He figured he could outsmart the game by changing the rules. But when the shit hit the fan, it came so hard and fast he wasn't prepared for it. He couldn't handle and made some careless mistakes. I'm not saying every move he made was a bad move, it's just that some of the things he did caused the negative feedback he was getting.

Cause and effect. I tried to hold him down as much as I could but I have my own set of problems to deal with, too, you know."

Craig shook his head and patted his pocket. "It's easy to make the money, but it's hard to maintain. There are way too many variables and you can't prepare for them all but you have to play it out when it arises. As far as you and him, I can't speak on y'all relationship and what y'all went through, but if you want me to keep it real with you, I can tell you there's a lot of temptation when you're in this game. That's why I don't have a girl today. I know she wouldn't be able to deal with all the shit in the end."

"I hear what you sayin', but there ain't no excuse, Craig. 'Specially not for a woman like me who held him down since day one!" Shondra said, waving her finger left to right.

"Don't get me wrong, Shondra. I'm not condoning shit he may have done. Look, I'm gonna tell you something you probably won't agree with, much less understand. A dude can have a girl and love the ground she walks on. He will treat her right and take care of her but he can fuck another broad and it won't mean shit; to him it will all be physical—"

"That's bullshit, Craig." Shondra interrupted. "Then a female can do the same thing, too. But if she does, she's considered a hoe or something even lower than that."

"Hold on, Shondra. It's different for a dude; we love with our heart not with our dicks. A dude can fuck a broad without much effort, all he has to do is pull down his zipper and poke around in her hole and after 50 pumps he's done. There is no love involved, for him it's just a nut," Craig said.

"A female can do that shit, too, Craig. That shit you sayin' ain't right; it goes both ways," Shondra replied.

"True, but like you said, if a female does what a man does she'll be labeled a hoe. The reality is this, Shondra: that's what hoes do. They fuck for sport with no conscious, a hooker does the same but her reward is monetary. She don't give a fuck about the trick, she only cares if his pockets is deep. To be honest, that's how a dude that has a main girl sees a piece of ass he wants to fuck: she ain't wife material, she just something he may want to hit from time to time. Ain't no love involved in that shit," Craig said, getting off the hood of the Benz.

"Craig, I didn't come here to debate how men justify their cheating. I came over to find Junior or find out how he's doing. I know guys stick together when it comes to cheating so I'ma leave this shit alone. What you're saying sounds typical and one-sided on how men think." Shondra waved her hand. "Y'all think that if you take care of a girl that she can be your doormat; she must cook, clean, wash your dirty drawers, and accept the bullshit you shovel out to her daily. That shit is for a weak bitch! Anything a man can do a woman can do, too. That's the bottom line. Call her a whore, call her a slut, call her a bitch, but make sure you emphasize the Ms. in front of it." She rolled her neck and continued. "If I did what Junior did to me, he would be ready to kill me. But since he does it and gives a lame-ass excuse, I'm supposed to sit back and be the good little woman and accept it. Bullshit, Craig, all bullshit! I can do the same thing a guy does!"

"Aight, I understand what you're saying, but realistically, you can't do what a man does.

"Aight, check it. How many babies can you have in nine months?" Craig asked.

"One," Shondra replied quickly.

"Aight, a dude can make ninety babies in nine months. Do you see the difference? What I'm trying to tell you is that there is a difference in our physical makeup, which also shows our thinking and reactions to certain situations is different too. We are all built different and what you do as a woman will be viewed differently than what I do as a man," Craig explained.

"There you go with that bullshit," Shondra smirked. "OK, so you saying since you can have 90 babies in 9 months, that gives you the right to go out and make them? Come on, Craig, what you're trying to do is justify why men fuck up in their relationships. I feel like this: if a guy don't want to be in a relationship, he should just say so and leave the bitch alone. That way it won't come as a shock to her when she see him with someone else and the same will go for him. If he sees her with someone else, he shouldn't want to flip out and beat on her."

"OK. We ain't gonna agree on this, so I'ma stop while I'm ahead," Craig said, giving up.

"I'm sorry, Craig. I didn't even come over here for this. I was just hoping to see Junior. I need to talk to him; I really need to see him," Shondra said.

"No problem, Shondra, but I ain't seen that dude in a minute so I can't really tell you anything. Try beeping him," Craig suggested, checking his own pager.

"That's OK, Craig. I appreciate you talking to me," She said, hugging him then walking off.

A blue Chevrolet Corsica pulled up in the parking lot of Tompkins Project as Shondra walked back up Myrtle Avenue and Craig headed back to the bodega. Junior exited the car and called out to his cousin. "Ay, yo!" he

yelled, keeping a safe distance in case Craig was still upset with him.

Craig turned around noticing his young cousin standing in the parking lot next to the car. He looked at Shondra who was just making it to the corner then walked over to where Junior was standing.

"What's up, boy?" Craig asked.

"Chillin' man," Junior responded, his hand outstretched to greet his cousin.

Craig looked at Junior trying to figure out if he was coming in peace or looking for redemption. Family or not, this game had no loyalty.

Junior noticed the look Craig was giving him and quickly spoke. "Look, man, I want to apologize for that shit that happened out here. I was buggin' and I didn't mean no disrespect to you. We still fam?"

Craig smiled slowly, grabbed his cousin close to him, and squeezed him hard whispering in his ear, "If you wasn't family, your heartbeat would have been stopped. I don't let nobody talk to me like that." He laughed in his throat and gently pushed Junior away from him.

"I know, man. But check it, I really need to holla at you," Junior said, getting straight to business.

"Hold on a sec, Shondra was just over her looking for you. She was saying she needed to talk to you," Craig interrupted him.

"Word? How long ago?" Junior asked, turning his head left to right looking up and down Myrtle Avenue.

"She just walked off before you pulled up. You might catch her if you go right now. She was actin' like she really needed to see you," Craig informed him.

"Which way she went?" Junior asked, opening the driver's side door to get in the Chevrolet.

"She was walking toward Sumner Projects," Craig replied, pointing in the direction in which Shondra was walking.

"Aight, but I need to holla at you; it's real important," Junior said, starting the car's engine.

"Go handle that first. I'll be right here when you get back," Craig said to him, nodding his head to someone who walked by.

Junior made a left out of the parking lot and headed down Myrtle Avenue looking for Shondra. As he approached Throop Avenue, he spotted her walking slowly with her head hanging low. He pulled up behind her and jumped out the car.

"Mooka!" He yelled out, using her pet name. Shondra turned around and was shocked to see Junior as tears rolled down her cheek. Junior walked up to her slowly feeling a slight bit of discomfort because he didn't know what to say. When he was close enough, she threw her arms around his neck and buried her head in his chest and began wailing.

"I'm so sorry, Junior. I'm soooo sorry. I didn't mean to hurt you, I swear I didn't."

Junior immediately became emotional. He didn't want to see Shondra cry and didn't want her to feel any pain.

"It's OK, Mooka. I'm the one that fucked up. I was buggin' out. I did a lot of foul shit to you and I'm sorry. I'm really sorry, baby. I didn't mean to hurt you," Junior whispered in her ear.

"Please forgive me. I made a mistake, I only told on you because I was mad, Junior. You know I would never do anything to hurt you…never. I love you so much, baby." She wiped her eyes against his jacket. "I missed

you so much. I need you back in my life. I need you, baby. Please come back to me," She begged.

Reality suddenly hit Junior.

"Look, Shondra. You know I love you right? But I can't go back to Baptiste. I gotta leave town. Because of what you told those police, they might try to pin that murder that happened in back of the building on me and I ain't trying to go down for that. Feel me?" Junior looked at her softly. "You fucked up when you talked to them. You fucked me up when you did that. Now I gotta go on the run." Junior's stare was serious.

"I know I fucked up, Junior. I know I shouldn't have told them pigs shit, but I was mad at how that shit went down. I didn't mean to, baby, I swear. I wish I could take everything back. I wish I never said anything." Shondra continued to wail.

"Mooka, all that don't matter right now, what's done is done. Now I have to do what I gotta do," Junior said, remaining focused.

"Then what's up with us, Junior? What about me and you? Is there still a me and you? You just gonna leave me alone like that? I told you I was sorry. I can go wherever you go Junior, I don't have to be in Baptiste, I'll go anywhere in the world with you," Shondra pleaded.

"I know, baby but I gotta get my shit together first. That's why I came over here to see my cousin. I need to get my money back right before I can take you anywhere with me. I don't want you to be on the run with me and go through the struggle. I love you too much to put you through that."

"I don't care about a struggle, Junior, as long as we're together. I was there before the money, remember? I can handle any struggle with you. I also realized that I

have to be able to forgive you and try to understand what you were going through for us to move forward." Her eyes showed sincerity.

"Yea, but its different now. I'm gonna be on the run and I don't want you to get caught up in the mix of that shit."

"What are you saying, Junior? You saying you don't want me with you anymore? You really want us to be over, just like that?" Shondra's heart was breaking.

"No, no, that's not what I'm saying. Let me get settled first. It won't take me long and I'll send for you. That's my word." His words danced off his tongue.

Shondra looked at Junior and although she wanted to believe him she just couldn't.

Junior saw the doubt in Shondra's eyes but had to keep it real with himself. Too much had happened and he had to secure his freedom first and foremost.

"Come with me." He grabbed her hand and led her to the car, opening the passenger side for her to sit down. He got into the driver's seat and headed back to the parking lot.

Junior held Shondra's hand in his one hand while he steered the vehicle with the other. She was gazing out the window wondering what was to become of his relationship with her. He pulled the car into the parking lot and backed into a parking space.

"Wait right here for a minute while I talk to my cousin," Junior told Shondra before exiting the vehicle.

"OK, Junior," she replied sheepishly.

Craig was standing in the parking lot speaking to the same Spanish girl when Shondra walked up on him earlier. Junior approached them and stood within earshot until Craig turned his attention to him.

"What's up? Everything straight with you and Shondra?" Craig asked.

"Not really, but it will be," Junior replied.

"So what's good wit' you?" Craig asked, telling the Spanish chick he would see her later. She walked away with a look of disdain on her face.

"I need a big favor from you," Junior said once the Spanish girl was out of earshot.

"I hope it's worth it because that's the second time I sent that pussy away today," Craig said smirking.

"For both of us, it should be," Junior replied.

"So what's the big favor?" Craig asked, suddenly interested.

"It's like this, cuz. I got a lot of heat on me from the Ds trying to link me to the body they found behind one of the buildings in Baptiste and I want to leave town before they catch up to me," Junior said.

"They sure it's you now? I'm saying…they let you go after they had you and if they had anything on you, your ass woulda neva came out of lockup," Craig replied.

Junior wasn't going to tell Craig Shondra snitched on him about the shoot out he had with La. He already knew how Craig felt about snitches and it wouldn't matter who it was. Silencing them would be his solution. Period.

"I know but I heard they been coming around there looking for me so I just wanna dip out and get gone before they get lucky and snatch me up on a humble," Junior said, looking back to the car at Shondra.

"Aight, I hear you, cuz. So where you plan on going?" Craig looked at a female that walked pass them winking her eye.

"Down South, to Aunt May's town," Junior revealed.

"That small-ass town? What the fuck you gonna do down there?" Craig asked.

"That's what I need to talk to you about. I got a little money saved up to cop a big eighth but I want to go down with at least a half a key so I don't have to come right back to re-up. I need you to spot me the rest and I'll give it right back when I come to cop again," Junior proposed.

"What you mean you only got a little bit of money? You should have more than just enough to cop a big eighth. Shit, you been hustlin' for a minute; you should definitely have more than that. What the fuck was you doing with all that money you was making? I know you wasn't trickin'?" Craig cocked his head.

"Nah, I wasn't trickin'." Junior turned back and looked at the car to make sure Shondra couldn't hear his conversation then continued, "But I been spending money 'cause I'm staying with Muffin. I gotta hit her off wit' some dough for me eating and sleeping in her crib. Plus, I ain't been doing my thing in Baptiste ever since Rock got bodied," Junior explained.

"How you know you can move shit down there? You been down there already?" Craig quizzed.

"Nah, but I spoke to our cousin, Bo, and he told me if I came down with something, he'll help me get rid of it."

"Well if you got it all figured out then, do you fam. I'll give you the dough to cop the half but it's going to be a one-time thing. When you plan on breaking out?" Craig agreed but wasn't really feeling Junior's plan.

"As soon as I get that half, I'm out," Junior said, smiling from the good news.

"Aight, I'll bring you the ends and you can go take care of your business." Craig walked off toward his building as Junior walked to his car.

"You sleep, Shondra?" Junior asked, sitting in the driver's seat.

"Uh uh," She replied sleepily.

"I'm waiting on Craig to get me something and then we can go, aight?" Junior told her.

"You don't have to rush; I'll wait," she replied.

"You have to be home anytime soon?" Junior asked her.

"Come on now, baby, you know I go as I please."

"That's good because we have a lot to talk about," Junior informed her.

"I know and I hope when we talk it will be about us fixing our relationship because that's what's important to me. Nothing else matters to me right now," Shondra admitted.

Shondra leaned over and kissed Junior on his lips with so much passion his dick got hard immediately. He instinctively groped her breasts, returning her passion. Her moans were turning him on as he continued fondling her breasts through her shirt. Craig knocked on the window while the couple was in the midst of kissing.

"Ay yo, you want this or you want to go upstairs to my room?" Craig said, holding up a black bag.

Junior and Shondra stopped abruptly. Shondra seemed slightly embarrassed but Junior didn't care, his concentration was on the bag dangling from Craig's hand containing the money he needed.

"Let me go handle this real quick and then we can finish what we was about to start," Junior told her, jumping out the car.

"I did you a li'l better than you asked in there," Craig said, handing Junior the bag. "All I want is what the key cost and 20 percent PC on top of that. You should be able to blow from there. That's a lot of dough, so you better be careful when you go cop. I want mine no matter what, cuzzo." Craig said seriously.

"I hear you, cuz. Thanks," Junior said, slapping his cousin five and pulling him in for an embrace.

"Don't thank me 'til you get back on your feet," Craig told him.

"No doubt. I'm goin' to bubble with this. That's my word, cuz, I ain't gonna fall for no more dumb shit neither. I learned some valuable shit being in this game and the hardest thing for me to understand is the fucking disloyalty, it's like you can't trust a muhfucka for shit!" Junior was speaking from his heart.

"That's what I been telling you, cuz. You can't let your left hand know what your right hand is doing," Craig co-signed.

"I know that now. You want to know something else, cuz? I learned that even the one you love will hurt you in the long run. Love is Pain," Junior stated.

"Hold on, cuz, you brought that shit on yourself. I told you I don't stand no disrespect from any man…period!" Craig retorted, defending himself.

"I wasn't talkin' 'bout you, cuz; I was talking more personal," Junior said, motioning toward the car.

"Oh, OK. I'm not gonna touch that cause that's between you and your girl. You got a lot on your hands with that one. She got a strong mind, kid." Craig said, waving his hand and chuckling.

"Aight, Craig, I'm 'bout to be out. Soon as I get down there I'm a holla," Junior said, walking to the car.

"Cool. Tell Auntie M to send me one of them pecan pies she always baking," Craig said, walking away.

Junior cranked up the car and pulled out the parking lot as Shondra stared at him with a distant look in her eyes. He turned the radio on and cruised down Myrtle toward downtown Brooklyn while Father MC's "Treat Em Like They Want To Be Treated" blared through the ten-inch car speakers.

"You want to spend the night with me?" he turned and asked Shondra as the car passed a red light on Classon Avenue.

"Of course, baby. I want to spend the rest of my nights with you," Shondra replied lovingly.

"You know I love you, right?" Junior asked, maneuvering through traffic and staring into Shondra's eyes.

"To be honest Junior, I don't know anymore. I mean, I feel in my heart you still love me, but my mind is telling me something different," Shondra said honestly, looking out the passenger-side window to avoid eye contact.

"I don't want you to feel like that, Shondra. I want you to know that I really love you and want us to be together," Junior said sincerely.

Junior's mind was going in a thousand directions and his emotions were getting the best of him. What he was saying was the truth but he wasn't processing things right; there were too many things he needed to clear up before even thinking about being with Shondra.

"Junior, you know that's the only thing I want. The only thing I ever wanted was for us to be together forever." Shondra looked down at the light spot on her finger where the engagement ring Junior had given her had once been.

"I'm going to make this happen. Trust me. I'm not going to take any more losses and I'm gonna blow up like I did before," Junior said confidently.

"Junior," Shondra asked, "do you remember when you said I never told you to stop what you were doin', the last time we spoke on the phone?"

"Yea," He replied.

"Well, I thought about that when you said it and you're right. I never asked you to stop because I didn't want you to feel like I didn't support you. But now I want to tell you that you shouldn't hustle anymore, you don't need to do it anymore. Let's just go away and start a life together. We can both find a job and work and live a normal life without all the bullshit hustling brings. Let's just be a normal couple, baby. I don't care about how much money you make or about you blowing up; my only concern is you and you alone."

Junior looked at Shondra briefly. He could tell she was serious by the look in her eyes.

"Just let me make enough money to make sure we'll be alright when we make this move. It won't take me long," Junior said to her.

Shondra bowed her head in defeat. "OK, Junior, I'm down with whatever as long as you're not lying to me."

"Trust me, baby, I'm not lying," he responded, exiting off the Brooklyn Bridge and heading toward Riverside Drive.

After about fifteen minutes of driving through the city traffic, the car pulled up in front of the exclusive Marriot Marquis hotel on Twelfth Avenue. Junior grabbed the black bag Craig had given him and went to the passenger side to let Shondra out. They walked into the lobby and Junior went to the desk to pay for a room.

Shondra walked over to the elevators and waited for him to get the key. They rode up to the seventh floor and entered the suite. Junior flopped onto the King size bed and breathed out a heavy sigh.

"What's wrong, baby?" Shondra asked, sitting on the edge of the bed.

"It just feels like a weight's been lifted off my shoulder," he replied, grabbing her hands and pulling her to him.

Shondra lay next to him and although it had been some months since she had been with him intimately, she could tell there was something bothering him. She was certain he was stressed out about the police looking for him but there was something else. She hoped it didn't have anything to do with that bitch, Muffin.

"I hope us just being together will take a lot of things off your mind…at least for the time being," she said, rubbing his head gently.

Junior closed his eyes, enjoying her gentle touch. It felt like old times and he missed what they once shared. Shondra was his real first love and he couldn't shake that emotion. But he had fallen in love with Muffin and didn't know how he would be able to handle both situations. Muffin had been there for him most recently while he was going through all the drama in his life. Shondra was a veteran and had been there before it all started and still wanted to be there for him but made a crucial error in judgment when she snitched on him. There was no way he could forgive her for that. Suppose she got mad like that again? Would she snitch again or did she learn her lesson? Even in love, loyalty was something you could not guarantee no matter who you were dealing with. As his

mind was immersed in deep thought, he unconsciously blinked his eyes slowly.

"Junior, Junior?" Shondra whispered in his ears. "Don't go to sleep yet, baby. I want to spend every waking moment with you."

Junior got up off the bed and grabbed a menu that was on the cherrywood desk and opened it.

"You hungry?" he asked her.

"Yea, for you," she replied seductively. It had been a long time since they had been together but the fire and passion they felt for each other still burned deep inside them.

Junior put down the menu and walked over to where Shondra was sitting on the bed. He stood in front of her and looked lovingly into her eyes. She felt her heart rate increase slightly from anticipation. He kneeled down in front of her and removed her Nike Air Max sneakers, massaging both of her feet gently through the sheer leggings she wore. His hands groped her calves through the silk pants then he made his way to her thighs, squeezing them softly as he became aroused by her heavy breathing. He loosened the silk belt that needed no help in holding her pants up, due to her round ass then he slowly peeled them down to her ankles. Shondra assisted by lifting her butt off the bed so the pants would go pass her ass and thighs easily. She hissed when she felt his warm wet kisses on her inner thighs. He licked both thighs and sucked them, leaving faint red passion marks in his wake while she grabbed his ears and played with them. He spread her legs and licked her soft middle through her black lace panties as she squirmed in delight. He could taste her sticky moistness through the lace and nibbled on her clit, putting his hands under her ass and squeezing

them like two ripe tomatoes. Shondra pushed her pelvic region into his warm mouth, hungry for him to take her. Her pussy jumped as he took one of his hands and moved her panty to the side and slid his wet tongue inside her pulsating tunnel.

“UGHH!” she groaned in her throat.

Junior looked up at her as she removed her silk shirt and bra then began squeezing both breasts. She rotated her hips slowly and pinched her nipples gently. Her hole was wet, mixed with her love fluid and Junior’s saliva. He licked her clit slowly, sucking it and making circles around the tip with his tongue, sending electric shockwaves through her sexual region. He let his hand wander up to her erect nipples and pinched them softly. He continued to lap at her clit, periodically sucking it then holding it in his wet mouth while letting his tongue flicker on it rapidly. The scent of her sex made his shaft harden and he rubbed himself hard against the mattress, increasing his arousal level. He slowly pulled back from her and stood up, his mass arching and protruding from his midsection like an iron C-Clamp.

“Fuck me, daddy.” she whimpered, spreading her legs as wide as she could as an invitation to him.

He mounted her slowly, grabbing his pole and rubbing it up and down her slippery middle. She moved her body to where he was trying to insert himself into her waiting hole but he kept moving his dick away, teasing her. He wanted her to wait and get the full effect once he entered her. His bulging cock then slipped into her hole freely from her natural lubricant.

“UGGHH…mmmm,” she purred, as her inner walls gripped his muscle.

He pumped in her slowly, watching his shaft disappear deeper each time he thrust.

"Aaahhh!" Her grunts and groans kept his staff hard. He pumped harder and faster as he became more aroused and could feel the tip of his head grow in preparation to explode. He pulled out of her and lapped at her sensitive clit, while he waited for his eruption to dissipate.

"No. Don't stop, daddy. Fuck this pussy. We miss you so much," she begged.

Junior said nothing; he just continued to lick her clit as her body squirmed. He turned her around so she would be positioned on her hands and knees then squeezed both her ass cheeks as she peered at him over her shoulder, waiting for him to enter her again. He kissed her ass cheeks and slid his middle finger in her gooey snatch.

"Uuummmm," she purred.

He wiggled his middle finger, feeling around for her G-spot as he squeezed her ass with his other hand. She began to move further up onto the bed, crawling and unable to take the ecstasy she was feeling. His finger went in and out quicker and quicker as he followed her to the other side of the king size bed. A sensuous feeling began to erupt somewhere deep inside her and her body began to twitch fiercely. He pulled his finger out and slammed his face between her ass cheeks while she lay flat on her stomach. He latched onto her clit and sucked it and let his tongue dance all over it while it was in his mouth.

"UGH!" she growled as her pussy collapsed, allowing her orgasmic juices to release.

"UNG, UNG, UUUUUNNNG," she groaned, losing control of all body movement and shaking like she was having an epileptic fit.

Junior slowed down to a slow tender licking as she wound down from her journey to sexual heaven. He stood up and looked at her lying on the bed, completely drained of all her energy. A few seconds passed before he slapped her on the ass with his still erect pole, signaling he wasn't finished. Shondra poked her ass out to him instinctively and he slowly inserted his rock hard piece inside her saturated cavern. She let out a low grunt as he went in and out of her with a methodic rhythm. Her body wasn't fully recovered from the orgasm but the pleasurable sensation increased with every stroke. After four minutes of pounding her from the back he turned her around and she lay on her back spread eagle. He entered her from the front grabbing her legs by the ankles for leverage and began longstroking her.

"OOOOuuuuu, yes, daddy" she murmured. "Mmmmm, yes. Fuck this pussy. It's yours, daddy, all yours."

Junior continued thrusting his hardened pipe inside her and tried to control his impending orgasm but her moans, squeals, and dirty talk was difficult to tune out.

"Come on, daddy, take this pussy. Gimme all that dick. Come on, daddy, fuck this pussy harder!" Her voice was beginning to rise with each word.

Junior began pounding harder and faster as she continued her dirty talk.

"Yes, daddy, this is your pussy! Fuck it, daddy, harder…harder…yes,
baby…yessssss…uuuuummm…aaaaahhhhh."

She could feel the tip of his head swelling in preparation to erupt his hot white creamy fluid. She clamped her legs around his waist tightly, arched her back and began grinding against him hard, pushing herself

deeper into him. Her circular movements proved too great for him to hold off any longer and within seconds he felt that snowy feeling come over him as he exploded inside her.

“Aaaaaauugh!” he moaned.

It seemed like his orgasm was lasting longer than usual as he felt Shondra’s continuous grinding, attempting to drain him of all his fluids. She was going faster and harder, then dug her nails in his back as she yelled out, “Ooooohhhh mmmmmmmm.”

She had cum again and it was the hardest she ever came before. She felt like her whole body was being jolted by 1,000 volts of electricity.

“Junior. I love you so much, baby,” she whispered, releasing her grip from his back and letting her legs fall from his waist like a rag doll. He collapsed on top of her exhausted and kissed her passionately on her lips.

“Damn!” he exclaimed, “that was good as hell.”

“I know, baby, it felt so different. My body feels different,” she replied, breathing heavily.

They held onto one another and fell off into a deep after “after good sex” sleep.

Chapter 7
****Junior & Shondra****

Junior's beeper was going off but it didn't wake him. Shondra looked at him then slid from out under his arms. She went to turn the beeper off because she didn't want anything interrupting her time with him. When she picked it up, her woman's intuition forced her to look at the number. Although the number didn't look familiar to her, she decided to call it back. Her logical side told her not to because it was an invasion of his privacy and if found out, it would be another strike against her. But her irrational side prompted her to find out if it was that bitch Muffin; her gut feeling was telling her it was. The irrational side won and she looked over to Junior who was snoring like a boar; a small earthquake wouldn't wake him after that good pussy she put on him. She picked up the telephone on the desk and began dialing the numbers on the keypad. When the phone started to ring on the other end she became nervous. She was risking everything on this phone call.

"Hello? Hello? Junior?" The female's voice on the other end asked.

Shondra put the receiver down gently, ending the call. She raced back to where Junior had his pants and clipped his beeper back onto the belt. Then she eased back into the bed with him as if she had never gotten up. While she nuzzled up next to him, his beeper went off again, startling her. She hoped it wouldn't wake him now because she would be busted for sure. The beeper continued to go off every second like an annoying broken alarm clock. Soon, Junior turned over on his stomach, grunted, and then farted.

"I wish that bitch stop calling his fucking number," Shondra thought to herself.

Finally the incessant ringing became too much and Junior jumped out of his sleep realizing his pager was going off. Shondra quickly closed her eyes as if she was still sleeping and breathed heavily for emphasis. Junior slid out of the bed quietly trying not to wake the actress. Then he retrieved his pager and looked at the number.

"Shit!" he thought silently. It was Muffin. He tried to think of what to do as he turned the pager on vibrator so as not to disrupt Shondra's slumber. He had to call her back or she would become suspicious, but he couldn't chance calling her from the room. He put on his pants and was about to head to the door when he heard a groggy Shondra ask from the bed, "Where you going, daddy?"

He turned around and before he answered, picked up the empty ice bucket on the table: "To go get some ice, ma."

Shondra propped up on her elbows. "You still want to drink, baby?" She had to admire how quickly he thought on his feet like he was anticipating her question.

"Shiiiit. After that episode with you, I need to re-energize myself so I can tackle that ass again. You know it's been a minute since we been together and I'm tryin' to

play catch-up before I make this move out of town," he answered, grabbing the knob on the door.

Shondra smirked and said, "Don't take too long or I'll come out there looking for you, daddy."

"Don't worry, ma; I ain't gonna be long. *Trust me*." The door closed behind him and Shondra jumped out of the bed and put on her clothes quickly and went to the door.

"That was the third 'trust me' of the tonight. I gotta find out if it's real or not," she thought to herself as she opened the door slowly. She saw Junior as he rounded the corner toward the elevator. She figured he was going to the lobby to make the call so she went back into the room to get the key and ran back out to follow him. The red plush carpet in the hallway eliminated any sounds of her footsteps as she approached the end of the hallway. She kneeled down and peeked around the corner and could see Junior boarding the elevator. When the doors closed she went to the elevator and pushed the down arrow as she watched the numbered lights above the elevator Junior was riding in blink, showing each floor it passed. Before the other elevator arrived, she noticed his elevator had stopped on the third floor.

"Slick muhfucka," she mumbled under her breath.

When her elevator arrived, she got inside and pushed the button for the fourth floor and rode down until the doors opened and a faint bell sounded. She exited the elevator and searched for an exit closest to the telephone booth on that floor. After finding an exit on the south side near the booth, she descended the stairs and headed toward the third floor exit. She opened the door slowly, listening for Junior's voice. She could hear him but only faintly. She opened the door wider and looked in the direction of the

phone booths and could see Junior leaning against one of the booths talking on the phone. Her vision was partially blocked by an array of fake flowers situated in a vase in the hallway. She could hear him better although she couldn't see him clearly.

"…yea, ma, I got it. So pack some clothes, 'bout two weeks worth of shit, cause I don't know how long it's gonna take me to knock all this shit off."

Shondra couldn't believe he was calling another bitch "ma." That was what he called her. Her heart dropped. She couldn't believe she was hearing him correctly. She didn't want to hear anything else but her womanly instinct of snooping wouldn't allow her to leave.

"…uh huh. I'm still with my cousin. Nah, I didn't call you earlier. I didn't hear it when it went off cause we going over some things before I leave. You know what I'm sayin'? You know how muhfuckas get when they feel they money situation 'bout to change. He want to make sure this shit go right and he don't take a loss." There was a pause. "Yea, ma, I thought about all that. Don't worry about nothing. I got you. You know I'm not gonna let nothing happen to you or me. We 'bout to take this shit to the next level; watch and see," Junior said.

Shondra felt heat rising in the back of her neck and her palms were getting sweaty. She wanted to rush out and bust him but decided against it. The words 'trust me' rang in her head as she contemplated what to do. After hearing all the shit he said to another bitch, why would she want to be with him? And if her intuition was correct, he was talking to Muffin, the bitch that was the cause of the bullshit they were going through in the first place. How could he still be doing this to her? How could he claim he loved her so much then run down and return that bitch's

call while they were together? How could he make passionate love to her – give her the best orgasm she'd had in a long time then turn around and do some foul shit like this? Shondra's thoughts were racing through her mind like a VCR playing on fast forward.

"Aight, ma. I'll see you lata on tonight when I'm done with my cousin." He paused. "I love you too, Muff."

Confirmation. There was no more guessing: she was 100 percent sure it was that bitch now. She heard him hang up the phone. She closed the door gently and ran up the stairs with a burst of energy spawned by furious rage.

"I LOVE YOU, MUFF!" she repeated out loud to herself as she climbed the stairs two steps at a time in approach to the seventh floor. When she entered the room, she didn't realize she was crying as she took off her clothes and jumped back in the bed and pulled the covers over her.

Junior took the elevator up to the seventh floor and walked toward the room. When he reached the room door he was about to knock but realized the empty ice bucket in his hand. He quickly turned around and went to the icemaker to fill up the ice bucket. Once it was filled up, he returned to the room. Then he knocked on the door. Ten seconds passed and Shondra didn't open the door. He knocked a little harder the next time and waited. Finally Shondra opened the door, the sheets from the bed wrapped around her body like a Roman goddess.

"You want some more to drink, ma?" Junior asked, walking into the room and grabbing his glass from the table, filling it with ice.

"This muhfucka got some nerve!" she screamed inside her mind. "No, Junior, I don't want nothing." She sounded dejected.

Junior poured the remaining contents of the green-bottled champagne with bronze labeling around the neck then looked at Shondra out the corner of his eye. She was lying with her head facing the television and it sounded like she was crying from the muffled sniffling noises coming from her. He figured she was crying because he would be leaving and not taking her and suddenly felt bad. He took a gulp from the glass then put it down on the table and stumbled over to the bed.

"What's wrong, ma?" he asked, sitting down on the edge of the bed.

Shondra turned to him, the whites of her eyes turned crimson from crying. She answered: "Do you really want to know?"

He placed a hand on her thigh, "Yea, I want to know. I don't want to see you hurting."

She looked at him and searched his eyes for the love they once shared.

"Junior. Do you still love me?" she asked, wiping her eyes.

"Yea. Why you ask that?" Junior said, perplexed by the question.

"No, I mean do you love me the same way you loved me when we first got together?" she said, continuing to probe him for any ounce of authenticity.

Junior paused; he didn't understand the question. He knew he loved her but he couldn't gauge the degree of his love for her at that moment. His emotions were a smorgasbord of mixed feelings.

"Yea. I love you more," he replied with unsurety in his voice.

The look Shondra gave him could have killed 1,000 men instantly. He knew she didn't believe him but he

didn't know what he could do or say to make her believe him. She began to cry uncontrollably and he tried to comfort her by holding her close, instead she pulled away from him.

"Junior. I love you more than anything. I really want us to be together but I can't take you lying to me about how you really feel about me right now," Shondra said sincerely.

"I'm not lying, ma; I do love you," Junior stated honestly.

"I believe you love me Junior, I just don't know if you're still *in love* with me. We've been through a lot in the last six months and I'm confused." Tears were forming in her eyes again.

"OK, I get it. You think because you told the police about me that I don't love you anymore? I can't lie: when I found out, I was mad as hell. But that don't change how I feel for you," Junior revealed to her.

"It's not only that, *Jun-ior*. It's about that bitch you fuckin' with and all the other shit that's happening. I just need to know that you still love me like you use to." She tried to peer through his soul.

"Come on, Shondra. I explained the situation about that bitch." Junior frowned.

"Now *she* a bitch, huh?" Shondra thought to herself.

"She coulda got me locked up for murder if I didn't keep her in my circle. That's the only reason I was playin' her close like that." Junior lied.

"Come on, Junior. You really want me to believe that shit? You want me to believe that you was only with that bitch cause you was worried about catching a murder charge?"

"Fuck yea!" Junior boomed. "You want to see me get locked up behind that bullshit? Oh, my bad: you probably do. That's why you ran your mouth to the beast," Junior said, his forehead wrinkling up.

"That's not fair, Junior!" Shondra wailed. "I was hurt. You brung that bitch to my hood and *she pulled out a gun on me*! What the fuck was I supposed to do?"

"You wasn't supposed to talk to those fuckin' cops, that's for damn sure! Look, I'll straighten that shit out with that bitch. You just don't understand the kind of pressure I was under. I was trying to handle by B.I. but didn't have no one to hold me down. Rock got murked and my cousin Craig stopped fuckin' with me. I had to bring somebody I knew would hold me down—"

Shondra interrupted him, saying through her tears, "That used to be me."

"Ah, ma, too much was going on. You was pissed with me," Junior said.

Shondra wiped her eyes. "Just tell me one thing then Junior, just this one question I need you to answer for me…and please, just be honest with me. Give me that much. Are you in love with that bitch?"

The room got ghastly quiet. But the silence resounded Junior's answer loud and clear; Shondra heard it.

Chapter 8
Junior & Muffin

Junior was placing the large Ziploc bags filled with Café Bustelo into the fender of the rented Ford Taurus Sedan. He was struggling to get the positioning of the drugs right so it would be secure on his ride to North Carolina. Muffin was in the house packing the rest of her clothes while he worked feverishly to conceal the drugs they would be transporting in the vehicle.

After seeing Shondra and making peace with his cousin Craig, he had an adrenaline rush and his confidence resurfaced from somewhere deep inside him. He was still unsure how he actually left things with Shondra but he wasn't trying to concentrate on the negative aspects of their relationship. After they made love she pressured him for a commitment he was unable to give her at the time. The only thing he was able to confirm was his love for her but she seemed not to believe him. At the time, his concentration was on making moves in North Carolina and putting himself back in the driver's seat of his life. He'd been dealing with self-pity and bad luck and it was starting to wear him thin. His love for her didn't die but the reality

of what she did when she snitched on him did make him naturally feel differently toward her. Although the rational side of his mind knew her reaction was somewhat justified because of the blatant disrespect with which Muffin had constantly bombarded her, the street code of never snitching took precedence.

As he continued struggling to make the illegal stash fit snuggly, Muffin approached him from behind.

"Freeze, motherfucker!" she said playfully.

"Chill wit' that shit, Muff. You almost fucked around and got your wig twisted around," Junior said, brandishing the black automatic pistol he kept easily accessible.

"That's you, always on point and prepared for the worst to happen." Muffin was smiling. "What's taking you so long, baby? I'm ready to get outta here. My mom's in there asking a million and two questions that I don't know the answer to. When you done out here, baby, please go tell her something that'll calm her worried ass down," Muffin said, turning away and sashaying back into the house.

Junior looked at her and had confidence she wouldn't break under pressure, she proved her loyalty and dedication to him on the police chase. He finished securing the stash then got up and went into the house to face Muffin's mother. Ever since he fingered her that day in the kitchen he tried avoiding her because he enjoyed the experience. But he noticed she was uncomfortable around him so he steered clear of her. He didn't want Muffin to get suspicious. He sometimes fantasized about her when he caught glimpses of her in the house. Her body was tight and she still had the type of sex appeal that only an experienced woman could possess. Once he got inside the

house, he walked upstairs to Muffin's room where, to his surprise, her mother was sitting on the bed. Ms. Turner rose to her feet and addressed Junior abruptly.

"Where you taking Muffin?" Ms. Turner asked.

"We going out of town to visit my aunt," Junior replied quickly.

"Where out of town?" she asked, both hands balled up in a fist resting on her curvaceous hips.

"North Carolina. I have family down there I ain't seen in years and my aunt asked me to come down and visit so I asked Muffin if she wanted to ride with me. That's all," Junior explained.

Muffin walked into the room and looked at both her mother and Junior.

"Baby, did you tell her where we goin', cause she swear you kidnapping me," Muffin said jokingly.

Junior looked at Muffin then at Ms. Turner and couldn't help but get aroused, it would be an American dream to have both of them simultaneously, full disclosure.

"Yea, I told her but I don't think she believes me," Junior replied, looking at Ms. Turner's blank expression. In the back of his mind he wished he knew if she wanted him because he wanted to stick his pipe inside her instead of his fingers.

"Well there you have it, ma, straight from the horse's mouth to your ears. I told you we just going to visit his family." Muffin tried to sound convincing.

Ms. Turner looked at Junior, seeing the lust in his eyes as he gazed at her mouth forming each word. "OK, but you better take care of my baby and make sure nothing happens to her down there. I mean it."

"I would never let any harm come to your daughter, Ms. Turner. I love her too much," Junior said sincerely.

"That's very sweet, Junior. I just want to make sure she's going to be alright because I can recall a time when she was in a car accident and you didn't think it was important enough to tell me and I'm her mother. So I'm just making sure this trip is just what you're saying it is and that you're only going to visit…your family," Ms. Turner said, intending to make herself very clear.

"Oh, ma, stop worrying. Junior always takes care of me, and that incident with the car wasn't his fault: it was mine," Muffin said, grabbing one of her bags and heading downstairs to put them in the car.

Junior and Ms. Turner watched her leave the room then he went to grab her other bags to follow behind her. Ms. Turner went to grab a bag to help and both their hands grabbed the handle of one of the suitcases at the same time. Ms. Turner quickly moved her hand but Junior grabbed it and looked into her eyes, hoping to see something that would give him the green light to his fantasy. No such luck; her eyes sent no such message. Instead, she pulled back from him then stood up and grabbed a shoulder bag that was on the bed. She didn't speak and Junior grabbed the bag and made his way to the front door of the room. Ms. Turner walked behind him and he stopped short at the door and turned to her.

"Don't even think about it, Mr. Junior. As desirable as you may be to me, you are my daughter's boyfriend and any thoughts of doing anything that will hurt my baby is out of the question. So, please go ahead and forget about what happened," she said.

Junior wondered if he heard her right; she did say desirable, didn't she? That meant she did feel something for him from that night he fingered her. The timing just wasn't right at the moment but he felt the opportunity

would present itself again. And the next time, he was going to make it happen.

"You right, Ms. Turner, I don't know what I was thinking. But you can't blame me. I mean, she came from your womb so my attraction to you is no disrespect to her, it's a compliment to you." Junior ran his game smoothly.

Ms. Turner was slightly turned on by Junior's comment but maintained her composure: "Junior that's very nice of you to say but what I said still stands. You understand me?" She cut her eyes at him.

Junior looked at her body in the tight jogging pants she was wearing and eyed her hungrily. Ms. Turner met his gaze and used all her willpower to hold back from saying or doing anything rash. She brushed pass him and her breasts touched his forearm and he took it as an advance. He walked up closely behind her and rubbed his front on her soft derriere. She turned and with her right hand shoved him backward, not hard but with enough force to let him know he was playing himself. Junior was amused and smiled wide like a schoolboy with a crush. Ms. Turner continued down the stairs and turned once to look at him and saw him standing at the top of the landing with an erection. He was also burning a hole through her sweatpants with his eyes. Secretly, she was turned on but waved it off because she knew nothing could happen with the young stud at the top of the stairs, he was her daughter's boyfriend and that's where it began and ended for her.

Muffin was returning to the house as her mother was walking out. She looked at her daughter at that moment and immaturely wished it was her that was going on the road trip—not necessarily with Junior, but with

someone who cared for her as deeply as Junior appeared to care for Muffin.

At that instant, she realized she was a lonely woman who yearned for the companionship and comfort of the opposite sex. Although she was approached by men her age, she wasn't interested in their idle chatter about themselves or their meek accomplishments. She wasn't interested in what model car they drove or how much money they had acquired over the years. What she wanted was someone simple and attractive who genuinely cared for her but still had the lust of a virgin. Ms. Turner knew she was still attractive, with abounding sex appeal to boot, but her better judgment was swayed due to the loss of her youth. She wanted to live recklessly for a change. She needed to throw caution to the wind and be more daring and adventurous; it was her right. These thoughts heightened her erotic sensibilities and made her mind react to the adulterated thoughts she was having.

"OK, ma, I'm gonna call you when we get down there," Muffin told her mother, taking the shoulder bag from her.

"OK, baby, be careful. I love you," Ms. Turner replied, hugging her daughter tightly.

Junior was coming down the stairs with the rest of the bags and noticed Muffin returning to the house. He stopped at the door then turned and said goodbye to Ms. Turner.

"See you later, Ms. Turner," he said, eyeing her ambitiously.

Muffin grabbed her bag from Junior and placed it in the car. Then Junior followed her, placing the rest of the bags in the trunk.

Ms. Turner stood at the door and waved at the duo as they prepared to leave. Her mind wandered and she knew the thoughts she was having were improper and completely wrong but she was not feeling guilty anymore. It was her right as a woman to feel, to want, and desire the comfort of a man. It wasn't right that her attraction was for her daughter's boyfriend but the burning she felt inside could not be ignored. She was attracted to Junior on a physical level. There was something else that had her wanting him more than just physically: it was his confidence. When she told him nothing would come of the incident in the kitchen, he didn't back off; he showed more interest and his attitude was that of a person who wouldn't take no for an answer. She knew her attraction to him was a direct betrayal of her daughter's trust and an abomination to the sanctity of motherhood. But the feeling was too strong to ignore. She knew she was wrong and there was no excuse, not one that anyone would coherently understand and she inwardly fought with herself and prayed she would be able to handle the outcome of her decision, whatever it was. She loved her daughter but in the end, love, as she knew all too well, is pain.

Chapter 9
Shondra

A steady stream of zombie-like characters were starting to mill about in the back of Shondra's building. Since drugs were introduced in the Projects, the users frequented the back of her building to get high because the back exit of her building's light fixture was always broken and gave the area an air of obscurity. She was looking out the living room window as the crowd grew and watched as the flame from a lighter flickered on and off; the crackheads inhaled the smoke from their glass pipes.

She wondered what their lives were like before they started smoking the highly addictive drug, how they made a choice to give up their family and friends just to chase that high. The drug had to have some unknown powers to make a mother abandon her child, a man steal from his family, or a woman sell her body. When she and Junior were together, he sold the very drug she wondered about and she never actually thought about the effects it had on its users. But now that he was not an active part of her life, it seemed to matter all of a sudden. It was as if the blinders were removed from her eyes.

She was associated with it indirectly and it had an adverse effect on her personal life. Somehow it seemed that being around the drug didn't just ruin the user's life: it also ruined her life. She had lost her best friend and her man because of it. There was no proof this was the case but it was. She needed to make sense of why her life was turning out the way it was.

As she continued to watch the antics of the users in the back of her building, Chico arrived on the scene and served them more drugs. She hadn't spoken to him since he slapped her three weeks ago and was embarrassed because she knew she had played herself in how she treated him. And after finding out Junior was still lying to her about Muffin that proved their relationship was basically over. She had a desire to make amends with Chico; she didn't want to be alone.

She watched as he counted his money then left the area. She rushed to the front door, hoping to catch him as he walked through the lobby to the front of the building. She opened her door just as he opened the exit door to the lobby. He stepped into the lobby but didn't look in her direction; she cleared her throat to get his attention. "Uh hmm."

Chico turned toward the sound. When he saw it was Shondra, his face possessed a look of contempt. He kept his pace to the entrance of the building.

"Chico," she called out to him before he reached the building entrance.

"What!" he replied, reluctantly turning around to see what she wanted.

"Chico, can we talk? I…I just want to apologize for how I treated you," Shondra said to him.

"Aright," he said, raising one eyebrow.

"You have time to talk now or you're busy?" she asked.

He looked at his Movado. "How long it's goon' take cause I got to make a run to other side right quick."

"It can wait 'til later if you don't have time. I just want to talk to you." She said with great humility.

Chico walked toward her. "Aight, we can talk now."

Shondra didn't know what she was going to say to him. She didn't have anything rehearsed; she was being impulsive. She opened the door wide enough for him to enter.

"I'm not going in; say what you have to right here," Chico demanded.

Shondra was taken aback by his heartless attitude but refrained from reacting negatively. She was in a vulnerable state at the moment and needed comfort and to feel wanted again. Junior destroyed her trust by deceiving her. He fucked her in the hotel and lied in her face with no regards for her feelings. What she felt was beyond hurt. She was devastated and her self-esteem was damaged, perhaps beyond repair.

"Look, Chico, I want to say sorry for treating you so fucked up. I was hurt and took my pain and frustration out on you. I was wrong and I know that now. I know you think I'm a real bitch but I really do like you." She sounded sincere but a little desperate; her sincerity was a function of her recent experiences and she was left humbled.

Shondra looked into Chico's eyes and couldn't tell if he believed her or not. She was distraught emotionally and needed companionship to keep her sanity. She dreaded the thought of being alone and was frantic to feel the love and comfort of a man again.

She was genuinely attracted to Chico; he was a very handsome young man with his long beautiful hair. Her hope was to have him forgive her and then she would show him how she really treated a man when in a committed relationship.

The love Shondra felt for Junior was still present in her heart but the abuse was too much. She needed to feel real love once again. Her relationship with Junior spiraled out of control the first day she found out about Muffin. Junior left her to deal with what was available to her; Chico was the chosen one. She was hoping he would be the rock of support she needed to get over Junior.

"Yo, Shondra, why the change of heart all of the sudden? I'm saying, you was acting real crazy a minute ago and now you sounding all sorry and shit, what's this really about?" Chico asked quizzically.

Although she wasn't the prettiest flower in Baptiste, there was something about her sex appeal and the way she fucked him that had Chico's young nose wide open. Aside from her crazy outbursts, wild ways, and the fact that she fucked with Junior, she was sure he would consider dealing with her on a serious level.

"Do I have to discuss my business in the hallway? Can you come in or come back later so I can tell you without the rest of the Projects hearing?" she asked softly. Her eyes looked sad and empty. The way she held her head down showed she was surrendering herself.

"Aight, I'ma come in for a minute," Chico said, stepping inside the apartment.

Shondra breathed a sigh of relief as she closed the door behind him slowly. She tried to grab his hand and lead him into her bedroom but he pulled away from her gently.

"Let's talk right here in the living room," he said, taking a seat on the velvet couch where their connection originated.

"OK," Shondra said, breathing out heavily, almost dreading to spill her guts to a guy with whom she had no guarantee of a future. "Look, I'ma keep it real with you. I've been put through so much in the last year that I'm drained from the bullshit. I'm unsure of what kind of relationship I have with Junior and it's been like that for the past six or seven months. It had me all fucked up and bitter." She looked at Chico who was staring at her with what seemed like caring eyes. "I wasn't the type of girl to step out on any man I was dealing with; I was loyal to a fault. I felt that if I did everything I was supposed to do as a woman, then my man wouldn't have no reason or excuse to seek out another bitch."

"I've been this way for as long as I've had boyfriends, so I know I'm a damn good girl and deserve to be treated as such. I never had eyes for another man while I was in a relationship. But since I was going through so much shit with Junior, I started to take notice of things I wouldn't normally take notice of."

She looked deeply into Chico's eyes and he averted her gaze. "When I saw you, Chico, I was attracted to you physically at first and had to have you. When we first slept together, it probably was for revenge on my part. But over time it grew into something more serious. Now I realize I treated you so bad because I felt so guilty. I was confused and wasn't sure if me and Junior would get back together but I knew if he found out I was cheating on him, he would leave me."

"Chico, I didn't mean to involve you in my mess or treat you the way I did and I'm truly sorry. I want to be

with you. I just hope it's not too late and you can forgive me for how I treated you and give this a chance."

Chico looked at Shondra and blinked his eyes slowly. Shondra had just emptied her soul to him and hoped it touched him somewhere deep inside.

"So, you and Junior are broke up?" he asked, tilting his head to the side.

Shondra looked up to the ceiling, "Honestly? I don't know, Chico; I really don't know. I mean, it's like this: I did everything to try and save the relationship but he still lying to me. So, to me, I think it's over," Shondra replied truthfully.

"That's to you but what about what he think?" Chico asked.

"I don't really know. It depends on what happens with me and you," she responded, rubbing her hands on her thighs.

"What the fuck is that supposed to mean? What you looking for me to tell you?" Chico asked, scratching his scalp in between braids.

"Look, Chico, I need to know if you feel something for me. At least then I can make a decision on what I'm gonna do. I know it sounds like bullshit but I'm not the type of female to have two men. So, if you say you want to be with me, then I'll make it official with Junior; I will make sure he knows it's over between us," She said quite seriously.

"That does sound like real bullshit, Shondra. It sounds like you trying to hold onto him until you find somebody to replace him. I don't want to get caught up in no bullshit with that dude over you. He already came through here on some dumb shit before and it coulda turned out a lot different if I was strapped." Chico put on a

hard face. "You saying if I tell you I want to fuck with you like that, that's when you'll let him know it's over? How you think he gon' react to that? You think he gon' just let it go just like that. If he come around here and see me in your crib or see us out anywhere, he liable to wig out and do something stupid over you and to me it's not worth it. Straight up." Chico waved his hand left to right. "You saying you feeling me like that and you sorry for all that bullshit you did in the beginning but you still got that dude in your heart. That's the bullshit I'm not trying to be a part of," Chico said as he was getting up and preparing to leave.

"Hold on, Chico," Shondra said, standing in front of him. "He not gon' come over here no more because the police looking for him, so you don't have to worry about him coming to my crib. When I spoke to him last, he was leaving town, so he not even in Brooklyn; that's what I'm trying to tell you. It's already over. I just haven't spoken to him to let him know. If you and me start dealing then I will have to tell him so there won't be any problems for us."

"Believe me, I know what you're thinking, but I don't like that type of drama. If you my man, you my man, period." Shondra grabbed his hand in hers. "Yea, I still got feelings for him, we got history together, so I'm not going to be able to turn my feelings off just like that. But if I'm with you, it will help me get over him because I will make you the focus of my attention. I know you younger than me, Chico, and I'm not a little girl, I'm a grown woman, so dealing with me won't be like no relationship you had with those little chickens you be fucking with. You already know this, Chico, and you can tell by how we fuck that it's different; I know you know, papi." She squeezed his hand softly.

“Sounds like you just wanna use me to help you get over that muhfucka, that’s what it sounds like to me. Look, let me think about this before I tell you anything, because right now, I’m not sure I can trust your words. I want to but it’s hard…”

Shondra cut him off. “I know it’s hard to believe me because of how I treated you in the past. But that’s what I’m trying to explain to you. I won’t do that to you again, Chico. I will treat you like a man—my man. You will get my best, believe me.” Shondra pulled him to her slowly. She had never gone for a man like this before in her life, she was usually the hunted. It wasn’t that she was weak for a man: she just needed someone to cushion the blow to her heart.

“Aight, like I said, let me think about it before I make any kind of decision.”

“OK, baby, I’m not gon’ pressure you too much but at least let me know if you like me like that. At least let me know that much.” She sounded like she was pleading.

Chico stared into her brown eyes, “Yea, I’m feeling you like that.” He kissed her on her discolored lips then headed out the door.

Shondra stood by the door and watched as he walked down the stairs and out of the building lobby. Then she closed the door behind her and put her back against it. She was praying she didn’t play herself telling the young boy what she wanted.

La

This was the sixth female La had bagged since the week started. He was entertaining a different broad every day of the week and his confidence was at an all-time high.

Chico was bringing him more money since witnessing how ruthless La was after shooting Smiley on the roof. Money was plentiful and he didn't have any regrets, giving him time to enjoy his favorite pastime: getting new broads.

The week was almost over and he was about to break his record by having a different woman for every day. He was still staying with Misty but transformed the small project bedroom into a comfortable and accommodating haven for him and his conquests. He did the best he could with the space. He painted the room royal blue and put up light blue Venetian blinds for slight contrast; he also purchased an oakwood bedroom set. But he had to opt out of taking the two nightstands that came with it because he thought it would make his living space too congested. He kept the dresser and completed his media section with a 32" Sony television and an entertainment system consisting of a radio tuner, receiver, tape decks, amplifier, and CD player.

The slightly voluptuous young woman lay across the bed half-naked with only lace panties and bra on. La wasn't interested in having serious relationships; a woman, he thought, would only take away from him advancing in the game. The pretty bronze-colored shorty got up off the bed, took a Newport out of her purse, and lit it.

"You gon' take me home or am I spending the night with you, daddy?" she asked, blowing smoke out the window in the room.

"You wanna spend the night or you want me to take you home?" he asked, waving his hand to clear the smoke that didn't make it out of the window.

"Don't answer my question with a question," she said jokingly.

"I didn't answer your question. I asked my own," La said humorously.

"It's really up to you, baby. I'm good right here if you don't feel like driving to Queens. But I need to be home by ten tomorrow so I can get ready for work," she said, dumping her ashes out the window.

"That's cool, I'll take you in the morning then." La was laying with his hands behind his head thinking about how good life was. He turned to her and looked at her body then asked her, "You ever been with another girl?"

She turned and looked at him then flicked the cigarette out the window. "Hell no! Where the fuck did that come from?"

"Nah, baby girl, don't flip. I'm just asking. My man told me that a lot of females from Queens was into shit like that so I was just asking. Damn, ma, you all defensive and shit like I hit a nerve or something." La chuckled.

"Don't be funny, La. Just because I work in a strip club don't mean I eat pussy. I'm only a hostess there and you know it. You ain't see me take my clothes off and shake my ass on stage." She said in defense.

"Yea, not yet." He smiled seductively. "I bet you know how to, though."

She threw a pillow at his head. "You like them musty, pussy-smelling bitches that sweat all between their legs when they on the stage, huh? You just like the rest of them nasty muhfuckas that be throwing their money at those yeast-infected hoes."

"Aaah, how you judging them and you work right up in there with them? You 'posed to be better because you don't do what they do? I bet they gettin' that paper, musty pussy and all." La burst out laughing.

"They not gettin' nothing but a bunch o' ones, my tips are five dollars and better. I leave outta there with way more than most of them bitches make in a week," she replied.

"I really don't see how when all you serve is drinks. Maybe you bringing in more money because you do shit on the side." La blocked the other pillow that was thrown at him.

"You tryin' to be funny, muhfucka? I only fucked with you 'cause you came at me like you really wanted to get to know me on some real personal shit. So don't try and play me like I'm one of those pole-dancing bitches." She was getting serious.

"Hold on, you trying to say I'm the first dude you fucked from in that strip club?" La asked, his head leaning to the side waiting for the lie he was sure would come.

"Why you trying to make me sound like a hoe, La? Why you dissin' me like that?" she said, disturbed with what La was implying.

"I'm not saying you a hoe, but you acting like your shit don't stink and you work right up in the same spot as them bitches. It don't matter if you take your thong off or not, you still up in that spot. I'm keeping it real, mama and ain't no disrespect to what I'm saying. I respect what you do to make a dollar, but don't put down the next bitch for how she get her paper, that's all I'm saying," La preached.

"It's not that. I just don't want you to think that I'm like them. I don't want to be in that category with them bitches. I work there but I have some class about what I do in there. I serve drinks to the patrons and I socialize, but don't nobody stick money in my thongs, feel on my ass, or take me in the back for private lap dances. That's what

makes me different from them bitches, bottom line," she said, trying to make her point.

"And you asking me if I swap out, like you hope I do, so you can put me in the same category as those bitches. When you met me in the club, I told you I didn't date anyone that came to the club because of that same reason. I only dated you because you came at me different and said you would respect me as a lady and not look at me like a hoe just cause I work there. Now it seems you changing up because you don' hit the pussy and ready to see if you can indulge in some extracurricular activities with me and another bitch. I have to say I feel very disrespected and disappointed that you would even come at me like that." She got up from where she was sitting on the queen-sized bed and grabbed her garments off the dresser then proceeded to get dressed.

La didn't give a care about her feelings but didn't want to cause any bad blood because he wanted to keep her on as one of his regulars. When he met her at Destro's, the strip club where she worked. He wasn't interested in any of the strippers because he wasn't into tricking. His status excluded him from the regular patrons that felt they couldn't have a female as sexy or intriguing as a stripper without paying for it. Their game was purely for the dollar. He had the same purpose in the line of work he was in, so he was geared toward getting with someone whom he didn't have to spend money right out of the gate.

La saw Diamond when she walked by wearing a short skirt that came right above her thick thighs where her ass cheeks bubbled out. It left much to the imagination and he wanted to see her on the pole to see her ass in its full nudity, but she never went on stage. She was walking around the club serving drinks. La made his move when she walked over and asked him if he wanted to order any drinks. He asked her to sit down with him but she politely declined retaining her heir of professionalism. He told her he only wanted a drink if she sat down with him so he could get to know her.

Ordinarily, Diamond didn't go out with patrons and was used to most guys' persistence, but La seemed intriguing. She explained to him that her getting paid at the end of the night had no bearing on him buying a drink or not: it was her job to take orders for drinks. La laughed because he understood that barmaids worked off tips, so he told her to get him another bucket of Moët then abruptly turned his back to her. When Diamond returned, La was checking his pager and didn't see her place the bucket of champagne on his table. She walked away after waiting for him to turn around and acknowledge her with a generous tip. When he wouldn't turn around, she turned on her heels and went back to taking orders.

That night she secretly watched La from the corner of her eye and saw that he never moved from his table to tip any of the dancers and didn't even seem interested in any of them, no matter how seductively they danced in front of him. He even shunned the ones that were in between sets roaming the club looking for lap dances or private sessions in the back.

Toward the end of the night when she was getting off, one of the bouncers escorted her out to the street to catch a cab when she heard a horn beep. La flashed his lights and got out of his car. She recognized him immediately then told the bouncer she would be OK and walked over to his car. They talked a while and she grew more interested and wanted to know more about him. He invited her out to get something to eat then take her home,

since they were already in Queens where she lived. La's game was so on point that before daybreak she was in his house giving him fire head and fucking his brains out.

"Let me be a man and apologize to you, Diamond." He turned her gently to face him and cupped his hands under her chin. "I ain't really mean nothing by what I asked you, but when you started dissing them stripper bitches, I kinda felt like you don't really have the right to be talking slick about them like that if you work in the same spot with them. I don't think anybody should throw stones if they live in a glass house. I don't really judge people because I don't like to be judged. Nobody knows what the next man's struggle is like. Some muhfuckas would look at me and think I got everything and I do feel like I have everything but what those muhfuckas don't know is what I had to go through to get it and what I have to do to maintain it."

La pulled up the crispy white wife beater he was wearing and showed his wound. "This is what it cost me to have everything I have right now. It almost cost me my life." He ran his fingers over the scar, which started below his navel and stopped right under his rib cage, then looked at Diamond. His eyes lowered as hate seemed to emit from his pores. Somewhere deep inside his head, Junior was held responsible for the gunshot wound he now wore as a badge of survival.

La blamed Junior and Rock for what happened but it was unrealistic because the truth was that he was blinded with rage and the obvious didn't occur to him. His greed was solely responsible for the situation that befell him; his disloyalty and jealousy were the culprits to his unfortunate accident. Junior only defended himself and was well within his rights of doing so after finding out La was trying to set

him up and take over his spot. Neither Rock nor Junior inflicted the wound La sustained; Rock did nothing to him other than expose his lies. La's mind never processed the reality of his wrongdoing. He only saw what was convenient for him: the ridiculous idea that Junior was responsible for thwarting his plans and putting him in the hospital. His hatred for Junior, he surmised, would only die when Junior took his final breath.

Diamond stopped undressing and listened to La intently. He had some heavy underlying issues that weren't evident to her until that moment. Even though there was no relationship between them, she became a little more interested in the man that stood before her. She had inadvertently touched on a subject that was very emotional for him and she wanted to hear the story behind the gunshot wound he revealed. He didn't strike her as the emotional type but his emotional side did present itself when triggered. Yet his display of emotion showed his vulnerability as a man while still exuding power and confidence.

"Baby, I'm sorry. I didn't know. I think we got off on the wrong foot. Can we start over?" she asked, rubbing his back.

La snapped back to reality then shrugged his shoulders, "Nah, my bad. I shouldn't have took that shit so much to heart. You can say and feel however you want. That's your right. Let's just forget this conversation even happened. Cool?" He walked over to the side of his bed and looked for the bottle of Bacardi on the floor.

"OK, baby" Diamond agreed.

She played her position and sat back down on the bed and looked at La from the corner of her eye. This was

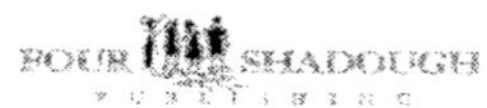

just their second time being together and she wanted to continue to see him so she was going to honor his wishes.

La pulled on his jogging pants and hoodie then laced up his beef and broccoli Tims.

"I gotta go check on some things. I'll be back in a half or so. You want anything while I'm out?" he asked Diamond, pulling his leather goose bomber from off a hanger in the closet.

"No, I'm good," she responded.

La grabbed his automatic .380 pistol from under the bed and proceeded to walk out the door.

It was cold outside but that didn't stop the flow of money in La's book. As long as there was product there was money to be made; crackheads didn't take days off. He walked to the other side of the Projects to pick up his money. He stopped by the corner bodega and picked up a box of blunts then continued on his way to see Chico.

Chico and one of the workers, Nano, were in the lobby of the building shooting dice to pass the time. Chico was boasting to the young worker about how he had Shondra sprung.

"Yea, and she be sweating me every night. Begging me to come through and see her. She be feenin' fo' ol' boy." Chico bragged. He got upset when the dice stopped rolling and landed on 1, 2, and 3. "Aced out!"

"Damn, you musta really laid your pipe game down to be able to take her from Junior," Nano remarked, picking up the dice and Chico's money, then rolling the dice toward the wall.

"No question. You know how you gotta do with them older broads. You gotta dick 'em down like there's no tomorrow." Chico laughed.

"I ain't never fuck wit' no older bitch before, but after hearing how Shondra been puttin' it down with the freaky shit, I'm ready to try," Nano replied as he smiled.

"I think them older broads like a young stallion cause we keep going after the first nut. Them older dudes probably not tappin' it right so they be looking for the young bloods to take over, you feel me?" Chico surmised.

"Just watch your back when you plunging, 'cause if the pussy as good as you say it is, I know Junior ain't just let it go like that. Keep that toast close by." Nano picked up his winnings and rolled the dice again.

Chico continued to brag to Nano about Shondra, lying and trying to impress him all at the same time. He never saw La standing in the back exit listening and watching both of them. When Chico finally turned around, he was startled and jumped. Then he dropped the dice onto the floor when he saw La standing in the doorway of the exit.

"Damn, La, you scared the shit outta me," Chico said, when his heart returned to its normal rhythm.

"What up? How's your count?" La's face was screwed up.

"I got it," Chico said, walking toward La while digging in the pocket of his jeans.

"Don't give it to me out here: come sit with me in the car." La walked past Chico then proceeded out the front building entrance, nodding his head to Nano.

"I'll be right back, Nano," Chico said to the young worker, who saw the quick change in Chico's character as soon as La came around.

La was already sitting in his car when Chico emerged from the building. Chico opened the passenger side door and sat down as La turned down the music

blaring out of his speakers. Chico handed La the money. La looked at Chico then turned up his nose.

"Why you talkin' shit 'bout that bitch to Nano like that?" he said to Chico.

"I wasn't talkin' shit. I was just telling him how she get down," Chico explained.

"I was back there listening to you talkin' shit like you macked her," La said, counting the money that was given to him. "But from what I know, she son'd you first. So you frontin', acting like you had shit under control from jump. You think them li'l muhfuckas really stupid? You think when you got pistol-whipped there wasn't a story behind that knot you was sporting on your head?" La cocked his head to the side looking at Chico then burst out laughing. Chico was offended but didn't dare say anything.

"Since you talking all that macking shit, tell me what you found out about Junior. And don't tell me you didn't find nothing out because you flying off with the mouth like you got her sprung on your ass," La said between clenched teeth.

"The only thing she told me was that he on the run now because she told him she told the police on him and his bitch," Chico revealed.

"She tell you where?" La's attention was fixed on every word that came out of Chico's mouth.

"She said he went outta town a coupla days ago with his bitch but she never said where they went. I don't think she know," Chico said.

"I need to find out how that joker movin' 'cause I don't need him poppin' up and catch me slippin'." La was speaking more to himself than to Chico.

"I don't think he gon' come 'round here like that no more since he on the run," Chico offered.

"I can tell you don't know nothing 'bout beef, young boy. When you got beef like me and that muhfucka, it's to the death. Ain't no squashing this shit, so somebody gon' have to end it so they can move around without worrying about getting caught napping. If I know that muhfucka: he gon' slide through and hope he catch me unarmed so he can finish me. I ain't going out like that so I'ma stay on point," La said, patting the gun tucked in his waist. "You gotta walk around strapped everyday; just in case somebody trying to creep, you even the odds. You can't think in slow motion or you'll be laying in a box looking up at the church ceiling."

"I hear you," Chico said.

"Do you really hear me, duke? 'Cause if you do, you'll be trying to find out where this dude at and when he coming back so I can take care of him. Who side you on?" La searched Chico's eyes.

"I'm on your side. You know that," Chico confirmed.

"Are you? It's hard to trust a muhfucka, 'specially when shit get thick and bullets start flying. I remember you bailing out when Junior caught you in the back of the building." La cracked his window.

"Yea, but he had a gun on him," Chico said in his defense.

"That's the main reason you should want to knock him off, too. You think if he see you again he ain't gon' split your wig again or even body you?" La asked.

"Yea, I know if he see me he'll probably try something." Chico nodded his head.

"Probably? Try most definitely. And you fucking his girl so he probably wanna get at you more than he wanna get at me. Muhfuckas act funny when they in love.

You should be trying to find out where he be at for your own safety. Shit, I know if he catch you with Shondra, it's lights out for you. Won't be no pistol whipping next time, captain." La laughed wickedly. He was instilling fear into Chico to add another pair of eyes that would literally be watching his back. Chico was all talk and wouldn't burst a grape in a fruit fight but with enough pressure he was capable of squeezing the trigger. A scared person would do anything to ensure his or her own safety.

"I don't have no gun, La." Chico spoke up.

"You ain't got no burner, boy? Oh, you already slippin'. You 'posed to got one soon as that muhfucka cracked your shit the last time. I'ma see what I can do for you on that but if I give you one, you better be ready to use it if you see that dude. You betta shoot first then ask questions later 'cause believe me, if he see you first, you only gon' feel fire."

Chapter 10
******Junior & Muffin******

There was no traffic on Carolina Avenue as the Ford Taurus cruised down the street. The driver's side window had been cracked open for the last two hours so the cold air could stop the fatigue Junior felt while driving down the highway. He fumbled with the radio trying in vain to find an R&B or Hip-Hop station. He turned right onto Boston Avenue and slowed down at a stop sign on the corner. Then he cruised through toward his aunt's house. Both sides of the street were lined with single-family brick and wooden houses with large, neatly manicured front yards.

There was no sign of civilization as far as the eye could see; there were no lights from oncoming cars and no sounds of life as he turned off the car headlights and pulled into the concrete driveway of the one-story red brick house owned by his aunt. The windows were so low on the house that if he left the lights on it would shine directly into his aunt's bedroom. Junior turned off the engine and got out of the car to stretch. He had stopped once at Maryland House, a rest stop island along I-95, so Muffin could use the

restroom and get something to quench her parched throat. After that stop he kept trucking only to stop to fill up the gas tank in Richmond, Virginia.

The cool air woke Muffin from her slumber when Junior opened the door. She sat up rubbing her eyes, trying to focus on her new surroundings. She was tired but excited as she watched Junior bending over, stretching his limbs. It was dark and she wasn't sure what time it was but it seemed to be the wee hours of the morning; it was so quiet she could clearly hear the leaves on the trees rustling in the wind. She grabbed the door handle and got out of the car. Junior looked over to her and smiled widely and beckoned her over to him. It was a little frigid but the temperature was significantly milder compared to the wintry December cold in New York.

"This is it, baby. This where we gon' blow up," Junior said, hugging her.

"Damn, baby, it's quiet out here," Muffin responded in a whisper, opting not to talk in her normal voice so as not to wake anyone.

"I know, ma. It's like there's no people out here; it's a big difference from up top. I used to love coming down here in the summertime. I haven't been back since I was young, but I remember we would sit on the swing over there and talk 'til the sun came up," Junior reminisced, pointing to an old wooden swing that was still useful but weather worn.

"Where everybody at?" Muffin asked, looking around.

"My cousin should be in the crib. I figured if he was up he woulda came out by now but I guess they take it in mad early down here. We might as well go to a hotel for

the night and get with him in the morning. What you think?" he asked Muffin, breathing in the fresh air.

"I'm with whatever. But I want something to eat," Muffin stated when the grumbling noise in her stomach reminded her she hadn't eaten since they left New York.

"There's a Hardee's around the corner from here. You want to go there before we go to the hotel? Junior asked, pointing in the direction he was talking about.

"What the fuck is a Hardee's?" Muffin asked perplexed.

"Oh, it's like their McDonald's down here. They got hamburgers and shit like that and they open twenty-four hours," Junior said chuckling.

"Aight, let's go then," Muffin said walking back to the car.

Junior followed orders and cranked up the car. He pulled out the driveway carefully and didn't turn on the headlights until he was in the street. They turned a couple of corners and pulled into the Hardee's driveway. Muffin and Junior ordered then left the restaurant looking for a hotel to rest for the night.

Across from Hardee's was a small motel, the Sunset Inn, which looked affordable for the few hours they would need to catch up on some rest before meeting with Junior's cousin in the morning. He pulled in and parked by the office and rang a bell. A short man in flannel pajamas who looked like he was from Bangladesh came to the window after about five minutes. Junior filled out the paper work, took the keys and went to their room

"Let's go get some rest, ma. I know you tired," Junior said to Muffin, as he exited the vehicle.

"I'm ready to take a shower. I slept most of the way but I still feel tired. I need to stretch out on a bed." Muffin grabbed the Horde's bags and followed Junior to the room.

Junior opened the door and encountered a funny smell in the room, like a damp carpet that was sprayed with hospital sanitizer to cover the odor. The room contained a single full size bed that was positioned on the right with a plain wooden headboard nailed to the wall and a wooden dresser with a mirror was alongside the other end of the wall. The wood was chipped and looked worn out. There was a floral print chair directly to the left of the entrance when you walked in. The carpet was a deep burgundy and had visible dark stains throughout. A small 25" color television was screwed onto the wooden dresser so no one would steal it and a touch-tone phone sat next to it. Junior entered first and Muffin came in behind him. He went to the window where some dingy beige curtains hung and flipped up a metal flap on a long air conditioner/heater right under the window, turning the dial to activate the heat. Muffin placed the food on the dresser then headed to the bathroom to relieve the pressure on her bladder. Within seconds, Junior heard a shriek and Muffin came flying out the bathroom.

"There's a big ass spider in there!" she screamed.

Junior walked into the bathroom to investigate and laughed. He removed the insect by its long legs and flushed it down the toilet.

"That wasn't no spider, it was a Daddy Longlegs. You know they got exotic bugs down here," Junior said chuckling, grabbing the bag of food off the dresser then tearing open the wrapper to devour his burger.

"You know I'm not used to that shit," Muffin replied, grabbing her burger from her bag.

"Nah, you not used to them, you used to seeing roaches playing tag in the bathroom," Junior joked.

"You a lie. You isn't nova seen no roach in my house, boy," Muffin said, rolling her eyes.

They finished up their food and Muffin took off her clothes and went into the bathroom to take a much-needed shower. Junior turned on the television and pulled off his clothes and jumped into the bed. As soon as his head hit the pillow he was fast asleep.

***

The loud knocking on the door startled Muffin and Junior out of their slumber. Junior jumped out the bed and rushed to the door and flung it open.

"You, why the fuck you banging' so hard on the firkin' door!" he screamed. The young white woman jumped when she heard junior screaming.

"I'm sorry, I was knocking on the door for about 10 minutes and no one answered. I just wanted to know if you needed your room cleaned or if you were going to check out," she explained, pushing her cart full of towels, disinfectants, and other cleansers away from his room to avoid a tongue-lashing.

"Oh, I'm sorry," Junior apologized. "I didn't know. Where I come from, when somebody knocking that hard it's not usually a house cleaner, you know what I mean?" Junior laughed half-heartedly.

"No problem. I'll be back later," she said, pushing her cart to another room and knocking on the door saying, "Check-out time."

"What time is it?" Junior yelled down to her.

"It's eleven fifteen," she responded as the next door crept open.

Junior went back into the room and retrieved the car keys and grabbed the suitcases. Muffin went into the bathroom to freshen up. He pulled out a change of clothes and placed them on the bed.

"What you gonna wear, Muff?" he asked.

"I'll get something when I get out, baby," she said from the bathroom.

"Aight, but we gotta hurry up. Check out time was eleven and it's eleven fifteen already," Junior said, putting on a gray Champion sweatsuit.

He picked up the phone and dialed his aunt's number and waited for someone to pick up on the other end.

"Hello?" the voice on the other end answered.

"What's up, boy? This me, Junior."

"Oh, what's up, cuzzin'?" Junior's cousin, Bo, answered, excited when he recognized the voice. "Where you at, mane?"

"I'm at the Sunset Inn. We got down here last night, man. I came by your crib but you wasn't home," Junior told him.

"I was here, mane. Didja knock on da do'?" Bo asked.

"Nah, I ain't want to want to wake Auntie up. I thought you woulda heard us pull up and seen those bright-ass lights in the front yard," Junior said, sitting on the dresser.

"My room in da back of da house now, so I wouldn'ta notice ya anyway. Who you come down wit'?" his cousin asked.

"Oh, I bought my shorty with me. You ready to get rollin', cuz?" Junior asked eagerly.

"I reckon so. It took you a month of summers to finally get on down here."

"I'm 'bout to check out. I'll be there in a minute," Junior said, ready to hang up the phone.

"OK, I'm here waitin' on ya," Bo replied.

Junior placed the receiver down just as Muffin came out the bathroom. She was looking scrumptious in her panties and bra. Her body was perfectly formed; she had a flat stomach and her hips were wide, giving her body an hourglass look.

"Damn, ma, if it wasn't check-out time I would have to get a quick taste of that this morning," Junior said licking his lips.

"This all yours, daddy whenever you want it," she said, turning around and palming her firm ass. She loved the sexual tension that kept Junior interested in her.

"And it's good to know you willing to give anytime I want, but first things first. We need to get up out of here and meet up with my cousin so I can get this shit popping with him," Junior said, grabbing his bags off the bed and heading toward the door.

Muffin was lotioning down her golden skin and pulling on panty hose when he returned from the car. She pulled on some tight Calvin Klein jeans with a cowl-neck sweater and a pair of beef and broccoli Tims. She was so Brooklyn at the moment as she pulled on her Polo ski jacket with the badges on the sleeves. Muffin was looking like she was ready to hit the block running. Junior was impressed with her enthusiasm. Her energy and his confidence were the formula necessary to make this move go right. He was going to put his all into making it come to fruition.

Chapter 11
K.B. & Gloria

The barber business was proving to be successful for K.B. and Gloria. The shop created a buzz. Not only were the barbers skilled with their shears, the female hairdresser brought a bevy of females into the fold, which proved to be a magnet for male patrons. There was another barbershop about three blocks from where K.B. was set up and most of the competition's younger customers began to migrate to K.B.'s shop because it was the hip new spot in town. New York Kutz was doing well in its first six months of business and was steadily growing.

K.B. and Gloria fiddled with the idea of opening up another barbershop in another town but weren't sure if they would be able to duplicate the same magic that made New York Kutz such a success so quickly. The energy of the consumers in the small town was something they hadn't anticipated and they weren't sure if any of the surrounding towns had the same measure of intensity.

Being a new owner gave K.B. the added business savvy necessary to expand his horizons, so he and Gloria traveled to some of the surrounding towns scoping out

prospects. He was particularly interested in Greenville, another town fifteen miles west of Little Washington. The population was slightly larger and boasted of more diverse hoods than Little Washington offered. North Carolina was seemingly untouched with new black businesses and K.B. had a vision of bringing fresh new ideas and capitalizing on them before it became too saturated.

The chime on the door rang and two young guys walked in. They took the only remaining seats. K.B. brought in more chairs and lined them up against the wall due to the growing number of customers. His barbers were now taking appointments to keep the crowd down in the shop; however, they did still take walk-ins. K.B. had a 32" television mounted in the corner on the ceiling far to the right of the shop behind the barber chairs for additional entertainment.

The two young boys who walked in came in on a conversation that was already in progress about who was the best rapper out. The toss up was between LL Cool J and Big Daddy Kane but there was also controversy over the new rap group, N.W.A., and what they were about to do to the rap game with their hard-hitting lyrics. K.B. listened as the barbers and some of the customers debated back and forth about where rap was going and who would still be around in the future.

You could always find some good conversation over at New York Kutz as well as some gossip. On the other side of the barbershop where Patricia styled hair, the women would give her the "minutes" on what was happening on the Block, who was fucking who, and what guy was making the most money. It was a like a regular gag fest in there at times.

K.B. usually opened the barbershop in the mornings then would come back around closing time and clean up then close up for the night. Gloria maintained the books and kept the finances in order. She wanted to be a major part of the business so she educated herself on the key components on running the business. K.B. was impressed with how she took an interest in their future.

They were currently living in a modest apartment complex that had many amenities, one being a swimming pool on the grounds. K.B. didn't want to stop there, he wanted more, although Gloria seemed pleased with their lifestyle. He wanted to live in a house they could call their own and was preparing to surprise Gloria with their first major purchase.

He had been looking at properties when they first decided to open the barbershop and now felt he was ready to go through with it. There was a large two-story brick house on the outskirts of the town, not far from where the barbershop was located. It was a colonial-style house with three bedrooms and a guest room, two and a half baths, a kitchen complete with an island and marble countertops, a two-car garage. It was all built on two acres of land. K.B. bid on it when it first hit the market and waited for the real estate company to come in at his price.

He received a call from his lawyer telling him his bid was accepted and to get the process going he would have to make the ten percent down payment to hold the property. He went to the lawyer's office one day after he finished up at the barbershop to write a check for the down payment and sign some papers. It was an exciting time for him; he could only imagine how excited Gloria would be when she found out they were going to be homeowners.

Gloria was sitting in the office talking on the phone to her mother in New York. She was telling her about how wonderful her life was with K.B. and how they were planning to come up for a weekend to do some shopping and to see the family. There was a knock on the door while she was talking.

"Come in," she said, turning around in the leather swivel chair. The door opened slowly and Patricia walked in.

"Hey, Ms. Gloria, I needs to run out to get some more supplies. I've run out and I have two more appointments," Patricia said, wiping her hands on her smock.

"Hold on, ma." Gloria removed the phone from her ear. "You feel you need to tell me this? Why?" Gloria said to her with a bit of an attitude.

"I'm only telling you so if my clients come in they will know I'll be gone for about forty-five minutes is all," Patricia replied, pursing her lips.

"Oh, baby, I'm not your secretary. You got this mixed up. You need to do your own secretarial work here, boo boo. You need to contact them and tell them yourself." Gloria put the phone back to her ear and continued her conversation with her mother.

"Can you believe the nerve of these country girls down here, ma? They work for you and act like you working for them…" Gloria turned her chair around giving Patricia her back in a gesture suggesting that their conversation was over.

Patricia left the office and walked back to her station seething. She was getting tired of the way Gloria was treating her. Patricia hadn't done anything to her, hadn't disrespected her and certainly didn't give in to her

so-called fiancé's advances toward her, so there wasn't any reason why Gloria always made it her business to let her know she didn't care for her. Everyone who worked in the barbershop could tell Gloria didn't like her and it was beginning to bother her. She didn't want to start anything because she wasn't the type. At the same time, she wasn't going to tolerate the abuse and mistreatment. If Gloria was insecure about her relationship with K.B. that was something she needed to address with him and not take out on her. Whenever Patricia had an early appointment and K.B. opened up the shop, he would always buy her breakfast, a gesture she didn't take as a come-on. But when he started calling the barbershop asking if she had eaten before he came to the shop, she became suspicious. Everyone knew Gloria was his girlfriend. For him to call the barbershop and ask for her directly, then show up with food for her alone, set off bells throughout the barbershop. In spite of all the nice things he did for her, Patricia never once let on that she was interested in him in any way; she kept it professional and never wavered.

Patricia was a wholesome country girl with morals and values instilled in her from her strong Christian background. Behind the innocent exterior, however, she was a normal female when it came to living life. She was secretive and chose her battles wisely. She didn't have a bad reputation in the street—her mother warned her about those "fast tail" girls in town. That warning taught her how to cloak when she was doing something considered unsavory by her family's standards.

She tongue kissed boys, let them play in her box and she even rubbed their privates, but she never went all the way. She was going to save herself for marriage because that was what a good Christian girl did. Her body

had developed early and she had explored her lower regions on many occasions in the shower and brought herself to full orgasm, although it was an abomination to please oneself. The feeling was so good she became addicted to fingering herself. She would pray for forgiveness afterward, knowing she would have to repeat the prayer again very soon.

She was the most sought after girl in town because no guy had the luck of getting her in bed. Even on her prom night when most girls lose their virginity, she was the only girl in her graduating class who didn't give in to her date's sexual advances. All the girls wanted Trevor, the star basketball player, but she brushed him off because he pressured her too much for sex, naturally showing his interest in being the first guy to hit it so he could claim bragging rights on busting her cherry. She let him rub her breasts that night and play in her middle but that was the furthest he got. Furious that he had wasted his night with a virgin who wouldn't put out, he left her in the hotel.

Patricia was still popular after that and the incident made guys all the more eager to be with her. On top of that, she was always the first to have everything from clothes, jewelry, shoes, to even the newest hairstyles. She was the envy of many of the girls in town and kept a clique of girls who were loyal to her. She never had to lift a finger to any of the girls who stood in line wanting to fight her.

Regardless of all her popularity, she was still the friendliest and most humble person you would ever want to meet. Her Southern drawl and charm would make any guy melt right in front of her. The sparkle in her eyes and the deep dimples in her cheeks were enough to make a man get on one knee. She was a pure Southern Belle, pure to a fault, fresh and untouched.

Patricia left the barbershop with a smile but underneath she was fuming. She didn't want to go behind Gloria's back and tell K.B. but she was tired of being talked down to and was ready for it to stop. She jumped in her red Ford Escort, started the engine, put the gearshift into first gear, and rose off the clutch too quickly. The car jerked forward violently just as K.B. was pulling into the side driveway of the barbershop.

"Ooops, I'm sorry, K.B.," Patricia mouthed through the windshield, as she put the car in neutral and lifted the parking brake. She quickly exited the car to see if she had hit his Acura Legend.

"No problem, Pat. You ain't hit nuthin'," K.B. said, waving his hand.

"I'm sorry. I'm just a little upset; that's why the car jerked forward like that," she explained.

"Who got you upset like that, babygirl?" K.B. asked in a concerned tone.

"I don't really wanna say. I don't wanna start anything," Patricia said, turning her head from K.B.'s stare.

"Nah, come on. Tell me who fuckin' wit' you," K.B. urged.

"I don't wanna say it right here 'cause they still in the shop and might come out and then it'll be a bigger mess," Patricia said as she looked in the direction of the shop.

"You wanna go somewhere else so you can tell me?" K.B. asked.

"Can you meet me by King Chicken?" Patricia asked, walking back to her car.

"Sure, I'll follow you over there," K.B. said. He got into his car. He had a genuine concern for Patricia and if he could play her knight in shining armor he was going to.

When Patricia pulled into a parking space at King Chicken, K.B. pulled in almost simultaneously. He got out of his car and spoke to a group of men who were playing a game of checkers near the far entrance of the fast food restaurant. He made his way over to the driver's side of the Escort and placed his arm on the roof of the car then leaned his head into her window.

"Now, tell me what's going on," he said, gazing into her eyes.

"Please don't get upset, but your fianceé is always talking down to me. I mean, she's nice when you're around, but when you're not there, she is so evil to me," Patricia said in a voice so seductive it would give a blind man a boner.

K.B. wasn't expecting to hear that; he expected one of the barbers to be the one harassing her. Surely, he would put him in his place with the quickness. But to hear it was Gloria changed everything. He couldn't honestly say anything to her without her being suspicious about his true intentions. It was evident Gloria was jealous of Patricia because she was fine as hell and brought a lot of business to New York Kutz, not to mention she made all men do a double-take whenever she walked pass them. It was hard not to look at her perfect, young body. He would have to come up with something that would appease her and at the same time make Gloria feel more secure.

"I'ma havta talk to her 'bout that shit. I be telling her to calm down with that Brooklyn attitude," K.B. said with conviction.

"But she only act like that wit' me. It's not like she's mean to everyone else: she singles me out like I did something to her and I have never said anything bad about her or to her," Patricia confessed.

"Don't worry, li'l ma, I'ma talk to her. I can see it upset you 'cause you nearly hit me when I was pulling into the shop," K.B. said eyeing her perky breasts.

"That's the same thing that happened last week. I almost got into a wreck when I left the shop upset after she had been mean to me again for no reason. I only asked her if she was leaving the shop anytime soon so I could run and get my grandma's medicine from the pharmacy. She flew off the handle talking crazy mess and I was so hurt and upset that I ran a stop sign and almost hit the back of a dump truck." Patricia was telling the truth but pouring it on a little thick for effect.

K.B. rubbed her shoulder and arm gently then gazed into her round brown eyes. He briefly fantasized about how it would be to feel her soft, naked flesh against his own. He wasn't the only guy who had a strong attraction to her. He saw how the guys looked at her in the shop and how customers ogled over her while she flipped hairstyles. K.B. was secretly jealous of those guys because he wanted her for himself.

"Where you goin' right now?" he asked her.

"I need to go to Greenville to get some more beauty supplies. I have to do some braids early in the morning and my next appointment is in half an hour, so I have time to go get my supplies before they close. I asked your fianceé to tell my client I was making a run if she came before I got back and that's when she started talking mean to me," she admitted.

"You want me to ride you out there real quick? You look like you need to calm down a li'l anyway. Why don't you leave your car parked here and get in my ride and let me take you to get your supplies. I need to pick up some things myself while I'm out there so we can kill two birds with one stone," K.B. suggested.

Little Washington was a very small town and any and everything that happened out of the norm was considered newsworthy. The streets always needed some gossip to keep the town buzzing with drama. There was hardly anything to gossip about, apart from the occasional shocking information in the newspaper of a young man caught stealing Kool Aid from the convenient store or someone getting caught writing a bad check at Belk's.

Patricia was no virgin to gossip and was sure the news of her getting into the car with K.B. would turn into a scandal. But she was armed and ready; it was time for payback and this was her town. No New York chick was going to come down and continue disrespecting her without feeling the country heat she could bring.

"OK, but I don't wanna get you in any trouble with your fianceé; you know how these folks down here like to carry bones," Patricia said, exiting her hatchback and walking over to K.B.'s car.

"Don't you worry about that bullshit. I don't feed into that shit and muhfuckas betta stay outta my business anyway. I don't play that talkin' shit," K.B. said firmly.

"OK, K.B., I'm just warnin' ya. I'm born and raised here. You just gettin' here. I know this town and these folks and they always itchin' for something to talk 'bout. So be careful. I'm not worried 'cause I ain't courtin' no one, but you have a fianceé and if she hears I been riding with you in her seat all the way to Greenville, it's sure to

be worse on me in the shop." Patricia was setting the playing field; she had to be certain she had K.B. where she needed him so her job in the barbershop would be secure no matter what happened.

K.B. laughed as he backed his car out of King Chicken's parking lot and jumped on 264W toward Greenville. He wasn't going to worry about all the blabber mouths in town because he had the ultimate prize in his car. He was going to milk all the rumors for what they were worth.

****Junior & Muffin****

Bo's eyes nearly popped out his head when he saw the amount of drugs Junior removed from the stash.

"Mane, we gon' take the town over fo' sho' wit' all this dope you got here, cuz," Bo said excitedly.

"This just the beginning, Bo. If we can bust all this down and get rid of it in a couple of weeks, next time I can make sure I have enough to keep us goin' for a month," Junior said while separating the Ziploc bags.

Bo was already on the phone alerting all his boys and users that a fresh shipment of coke had arrived and he had plenty of it. Junior watched him and made a mental note to teach him the same rules of the game that were taught to him so they would have longevity in their business. He could already see that Bo moved reckless by how he conducted business using the phone; that was a big no no in Junior's book.

"I need to find a stash spot for most of this stuff," Junior said to Bo.

"You can put it in here," Bo said, pointing to a spot on the floor in his closet.

"Nah, cuz, you buggin'. I ain't stashing none of this in the house. Suppose the police run up in here. You and Auntie going down. You understand that? I need to find somewhere where I can stash it so if they do happen to find it they can't link it to us. You feel me?" Junior said, placing all the work in one pile.

"Ahh, OK. I hear you, cuzzin'. You can stash it down da road over in da ditch behind da church," Bo directed, walking away from the house and around the back so he could show Junior the location.

"That's cool. I'ma bag up some work and we gon' hit the streets and bake this bread," Junior said with eagerness in his voice.

Muffin was in the house talking with Junior's Aunt M. She was amazed by her hospitality; she thought it was like being at home. When she saw Junior and Bo return to the house, she excused herself and walked into the room with both men.

"I know you don't think you was leavin' me in the house? I'm goin' everywhere you go, Junior. You might as well get used to it. I'm gonna be attached to your hip like your pager, booboo," Muffin stated.

"Come on, baby girl, I don't want you out there on the grind with me. Let me see what's what first and then I'll come back and get you," Junior reasoned.

"Negative, boo boo. I'm goin'. I'll just sit in the car. You not leaving me," Muffin enforced.

"Heh heh. See you gotcha hands full wit' yer ole' lady," Bo said to Junior. "You can bring 'er; she gon' be awlright. Ain't much happenin' out here, cuzzin'. I'm gon' take you on Ninth Street where most everybody be at," Bo said.

"Come on then, let's get outta here and get this paper," Junior said, walking out the door.

The Ford Taurus pulled into the parking lot of the two-story projects on Ninth Street amid a throng of guys and girls milling around parked cars talking and laughing. All eyes were on the trio who emerged from the car with New York plates. Everyone seemed interested to know who the out-of-towners were. Everyone recognized Bo and greeted him warmly as he walked over to a group of guys sitting on the hood of an old Chevy Caprice Classic. He talked to them while Junior and Muffin stood by the car looking around at the staring eyes of the people outside.

"Damn, I didn't expect to see so many damn people out here. Last night I was seeing tumbleweeds blowing across the highway, now all these muhfuckas popped out of nowhere," Muffin said, amused to see a large group of people her age.

"I was trying to tell you that. This town is small but they got a hood too. Anywhere you go, you gonna find a hood; it's a part of any city. They want money the same way we want it in New York. It's just not as easy to get product here as it is in New York," Junior explained.

"Yo, these girls down here look mad homely. They don't have hairdressers down this piece? I'm starting to miss home already," Muffin said laughing.

"Not everybody down here bums. You can tell the ones that's gettin' money by how they dress. Look at that dude over there," Junior said, pointing to a guy standing next to Bo, "he got on some Tommy Hilfiger jeans with a Tommy Hilfiger sweatshirt and a Nautica goose down. He rocking some nice shit but his color coordination is all off. He know the gear cost a grip but he don't know how to put

it together. That outfit probably came straight off a mannequin display in the store," Junior analyzed.

"Baby, they starin' like we aliens or something. They makin' me uncomfortable," Muffin reported.

"That's only 'cause they seen these out-of-town plates. They know we from New York but just curious to know what we doin' down here. Don't sweat it, ma. They mad friendly out here. You'll see," Junior said, watching Bo walk back over to them after talking to his friends.

"Ay, cuzz, my boys o'er there said meet them down the road. They want to see what kind of play you gon' give 'em for $1,000," Bo said, motioning to the group of guys.

"They want to spend a G like that already?" Junior asked surprised.

"Yea, mane. Ain't no dope down here. The town dry right now 'til Ole' Boy Cutter come back from New York. He the one that supply the town with all the dope," Bo informed Junior.

"Is that right? He sells to the the guys down here?" Junior asked.

"Not really, most everyone work fo' him. He don't sell nobody nuthin' fo' themselves," Bo explained.

The wheels in Junior's head were turning. He saw an opening that would give him a long run if he mapped it out right. He was going to make a power move that would prove he was capable of getting money anywhere, under any circumstances.

Juinor met with the two country boys who wanted to cop and they made the transaction. They had more money to spend but were waiting on their supply to come in, so they only bought a small amount to keep them going until it arrived. Junior respected their hustle but knew he would be their supplier very soon. As the day moved

along, he and Bo made numerous transactions for large sums of money and the count was enormous for Junior. His expectations were exceeded by how quickly it was happening.

Muffin sat by idly, excited and shocked at the same time. She never actually witnessed deals being made before, aside from when Junior took her to cop weight. To see the mechanics of the whole operation that lead to him copping weight was amazing and a turn on for her.

Junior and Bo were sitting in the back of the Taurus counting up the money they made and Muffin was sitting in the front admiring the country life.

"Yo, Bo, this shit is crazy man. We made seventeen gees already and we only been out here for five hours. Yo this town is a goldmine!" Junior was elated.

"That's because that dope you got is a killa. It's gon' fast 'cause folks hearin' we got the best dope out. You gon' sell out by tomorrow; I betcha," Bo said realistically.

"That's what's up. Let's go ride around and see what else is going on in this town," Junior said, hopping into the front seat.

"I'm gon' take you to a 'nother place 'round here where dey sell dope," Bo told Junior, directing him to the destination.

They drove about five blocks down and approached Fourth Street. Junior and Muffin were amazed at what they saw. There were crackheads and dealers making sales openly in the middle of the street. There were people scattered all over the street on the sidewalks and in front of a store called Moe's.

"This is the Block," Bo said matter of factly.

"Yo, these muhfuckas down here is crazy. They sellin' right in the street. What...ain't no police down this muhfucka?" Junior asked quizzically.

"Mane, the law don't mess wit' us down this end. They don't care 'bout dis mess down here," Bo replied.

"That's some bullshit, cuz. Let me tell you. Shit just ain't really hit hard down here yet. Ain't no real crime hit this town. But when it does and the police realize it's coming from these little rocks, then they gon' start bustin' muhfuckas down here left and right. Trust me," Junior said.

"You right, cuzzin', 'cause if we mess ova any of dese white folks, the law throw you unda da jail," Bo agreed.

"I bet they will. I'm not trying to get caught up with these fools down here, Bo. We gon' move different. These country boys down here ain't gon' last long in the game doin' that dumb shit there," Junior said.

"Let's get out right here and go in the Game Room," Bo suggested.

Junior parked the car on a side street and exited the vehicle then followed Bo into the community game room. As they walked in, almost everyone greeted them with a "Hey" or a "What's up, mane?" Muffin looked at the country boys and the way they were dressed and wasn't impressed. There were some females who staged her but she kept her head up and switched her ass as hard as she could. By her standards, she was the shit. Most of the guys were drooling and staring so hard it looked like their eyes could pop out their damn heads.

Once inside the game room, Junior immediately figured the spot was for the hustlers to take breaks and relax, sort of a shelter and place for downtime. It was a

cool little spot with a couple video games in the corner, a pool table in the middle of the room, and a freezer filled with soda and beer. There were a couple guys gambling on the pool table and some were playing the video games, while others were looking out the window searching for possible sales. Bo was conversing with a couple of the guys, no doubt giving them the 411 on what Junior was down there for. After clueing everyone in that Junior was holding, they set out to leave the game room. One of the boys shooting pool walked up to Junior and asked him where he was from.

"Brooklyn," Junior answered proudly.

"I got kin in Brooklyn. You know the Hodges, they live on Fulton Avenue up dere in Brooklyn," The young country boy said.

"I don't know, I might. But Brooklyn is big, so it ain't like I'ma know everybody, ya feel me?" Junior said, walking out the door trying to avoid a lengthy conversation about nothing.

They walked back to the car and eyes still followed them. It was as if they were celebrities the way everyone was staring at them. Junior added a bop to his walk and when he got in the vehicle he turned to Bo. "Yo, them cats be staring hard as a muhfucka, cuz. What the fuck is that about?"

"Mane, its rare dese folks get to see out-of-towners, 'specially from New Yawk, so they trying to see what you wearing and how you talkin' so they can imitate you. A lot o' dese boys out here wanna be from New Yawk so bad they try to change dey accent. It's funny hearin' dem tryin' to tawk proper," Bo laughed as Junior pulled off.

“What else y’all do down here for fun. I mean, is this it?” Junior asked, turning a corner and driving with no real destination.

“Well they have the Rec: that’s where the boys go to play basketball and foosball,” Bo replied.

“Let’s go there and see what’s happenin’,” Junior decided.

Muffin was in the back seat watching the scenery. She was getting bored just sitting around watching Junior and his cousin collecting money and selling those capsules by the Ziploc bag. She wanted to find some sort of entertainment; she wanted to chat with a cool-ass country girl instead of just sitting idle.

The Rec was a small brick building with an outdoor basketball court to the right of the building and a basketball court inside. There were a lot of kids inside sitting on bleachers, watching a bunch of guys running a full-court game of basketball.

“Damn, is there anything for a girl to do down here? All I’m seeing is girls following behind guys; it’s like there’s nothing for a bitch to do down this muhfucka,” Muffin said, getting frustrated looking at girls talking amongst themselves while watching the guys playing basketball.

“Ain’t much to do down these parts, we can ride out to Greenville and go to the mall out there and out to eat. It’s just not that much to do down here because the town so small,” Bo said sincerely.

“Be easy, Ma. We gon’ make our own fun tonight so don’t worry ‘bout that. Right now we just trying to learn the town aight?” Junior pulled Muffin toward him and held her close.

"OK, Daddy, I'm gon' hold you to that," Muffin said, leaving the gym to go sit in the car.

"Mane, you shouldn'ta brung your ole' lady witcha; she not gon' want to sit 'round while we get this money," Bo said seriously.

"Nah, she hustle with me. She just gotta get used to being in the South, that's all. It's a big difference from being in New York, trust me, cuz," Junior said, eyeing a girl with wide hips and a cute smile.

"You gon' have to be careful, cuzzin, these woman folk down here go for what dey know, so yo' ole' lady gon' have to learn how to scrap. Dese girls down here fight fo' sport," Bo laughed, paying attention to Junior's wandering eyes.

"Oh, my shorty ain't nothing to play wit', trust that! She lays it down and she'll let that iron go, too!" Junior explained to Bo. "She ain't no slow leak, cuz."

"I'm just jokin', cuzzin. Let me go holla at some of my boys o'er there by the bleachers. I ain't gon' introduce you to 'em 'cause I want them to come to me so you can feel 'em out."

"I like that, cuz. Do what you do," Junior replied, leaning up against the wall watching all the girls giggling and looking in his direction.

After leaving the Rec, Bo took Junior and Muffin to the Golden Corral restaurant and they ate and talked briefly about business, their family in New York, how he and Muffin met, and where they were planning to go after the restaurant. Muffin enjoyed her meal of teriyaki chicken with baked potato while Junior ate a well-done steak with French fries. Bo had a medium-rare steak with a baked potato.

"You ready to turn it in, baby?" Junior looked at Muffin with weary eyes.

"I'm ready when you ready, daddy," Muffin replied sheepishly.

"I got your room ready. You can have Billy Ray's room since he gon' off to the Army," Bo said.

"That's right; How long he been in there now?" Junior asked.

"It's been three years and he said he gon' re-enlist when he's done. You know he always wanted to be in the Army like poppa."

"Aight, well let's get goin'." Junior rose from the table and dropped a wad of one dollar bills as a tip.

"Mane, that's a big tip you leavin'," Bo remarked, looking at all the scattered bills on the table.

"I'm feeling generous; I made a lot of dough today," Junior said, smiling and grabbing Muffin's hand.

"You better be just leaving all that money as a tip," Muffin said, rolling her eyes playfully. "Let me find out you like them pink toes."

"You know I ain't never had a devil before so I'm trying to see if my money will spend," Junior said jokingly. Secretly he did want to have sex with a white girl.

As they laughed, they left the restaurant and headed toward the car. Muffin pulled Junior to the side when Bo took a seat in the back.

"I don't really wanna stay in your aunt house, baby? I want you to fuck the shit outta me tonight and I wanna be able to scream as loud as I want. I'm not gon' feel comfortable fucking in your aunt house. Can we go to another hotel, baby, please?" Muffin asked Junior.

"Not a problem, baby. Say no more." Junior kissed her on her lips softly and got into the car.

"Yo, cuz , we gon' stay in a hotel. Which is the best hotel down here?" Junior asked Bo.

"The Holiday Inn. It's right up the road on the right," Bo directed.

"OK, cool. You goin' in or you chillin'?" Junior looked at Bo in the rearview.

"I wanna go back on da Block and get rid o' some mo' o' dat dope," Bo said quickly.

"You ain't bullshittin' is you, cuz?" Junior said, bursting out in a hearty laugh.

"Aight, let me and Muff check in and you can take the car so you can get around. Just make sure you come back and pick us up before check-out time."

"Yo got it, cuzzin'" Bo replied.

When they were in the room, Junior pulled out money from both pockets of his sweatpants, his socks, and his hoodie. He threw all the money on the bed and began counting it. When he was done he had $26,650. He looked at Muffin and a smile formed on his face.

"I told you, ma. I told you I was gon' get it again," Junior said, looking into her eyes.

"No, baby, I told you you was gon' get it again," Muffin reminded him.

"You right, ma, 'cause I was down and out at one point and you was there for me. That's why I love you like I do. If it wasn't for you holding me down like you did, I probably still be fucked up," Junior said to her seriously.

"No, baby," Muffin said rubbing his back, "you just lost that feeling for a minute; this has always been in you. You destined for greatness, baby. That's why I stayed by

your side. But let me be clear: I love you unconditionally, rich or poor." Muffin kissed him seductively on his neck.

"Yo, ma, we struck oil in this town. I'm gon' take this shit by storm. They don't have no work out here like this. It's one dude supplying the whole town and I'ma knock him out the way immediately, soon as I see who he is, and I'ma rock out from then on. I'm gon' own this town before it's all done and over with. They move slow as hell and they move reckless, but once I show them how to move and get this money on another level, we gon' be rich with dough stacked to the ceiling. I'm feeling the love down here." Junior took a handful of bills and threw it up, hitting the ceiling and then falling as if it were raining money in the hotel room.

"You the man, baby, you the man," Muffin said flopping down on the bed covered in paper.

"Yea, I am the man: your man." He grabbed Muffin and kissed her passionately.

So much happened that day that thoughts of Shondra never entered Junior's mind. Muffin was doing everything in her power to keep his mind occupied but the way the money was rolling in for him, she didn't have to worry about it. The only thing that mattered at the moment was Junior getting back on his feet and her role as the girl who was going to be there with him while he was doing it. After all Muffin was doing with and for Junior, she didn't have to worry about Shondra anymore. Her position with Junior was as solid as a rock.

Chapter 12
******K.B. & Gloria******

K.B. walked into the barbershop carrying a bag from Belk's department store and spoke to all three barbers and the customers that were seated waiting to get their hair cut or shaped up. The barbers greeted him and some of the guys waiting to get a cut spoke as well. Then he went to his office. When the office door closed behind him the front door of the barbershop opened and Patricia glided in and walked straight to her station, right past everyone else, without speaking. It was obvious to all the barbers that something fishy was going on between her and K.B. even though they came in separately. Patricia emptied the contents of her bag and placed them in drawers and cabinets at her station. As she put away the items she periodically looked in the mirror to see everyone staring in her direction. She didn't care what anyone thought but didn't want them just staring at her.

"Excuse me, but do y'all have something you want to tell me?" She was looking at everyone's reflection in the mirror as she spoke.

"Who you talkin' to?" Jerome, the barber in the first chair, asked, ready for a confrontation.

"I'm speaking to the lot of you. Y'all staring at me like I'm about to perform on stage o' somethin'," she said sarcastically.

"Shiiiit. You walked in like an actress, coming in and not speakin'," Jerome said laughing, causing the patrons and other barbers to join in.

"That's because I'm a star," she said, turning around and shaking her ass so everyone could see.

"You ain't neva lie!" Terrence, the barber on the end, said.

"Sure ya right! I reckon you the North Star seeing how you come in shinin' right afta bossman come in. Ain't he from up North?" Jerome said, getting straight to the point.

"What are you trying to insinuate, Jerome?" Patricia said, focusing directly on him.

"I ain't trying to insinuate nothin'. Anyone wit' eyes can see you cloaking. It sure ain't a coincidence you came in seconds apart from bossman when he came in with dem bags."

"So what da hell dat mean, Jerome? If I come in seconds behind you, does that mean we were together? Please!" Patricia rolled her eyes.

All the barbers looked at each other then looked at Patricia who wouldn't match the stares she could feel were on her. Everyone saw her talking to K.B. when he pulled up and they left together. Then about an hour later they both walk in five seconds apart. That move had, "out fucking," written all over it and anyone with common sense could read it like an open book.

Inside the office, Gloria was looking through the bag K.B. brought in with him when he came into the office.

"Wow, baby, thank you!" she said, putting the sweater up to her bosom to see if it fit.

"I want you to put that on now so I can take you out to eat. You know I like you looking brand new, baby," he said, smiling and reclining in the chair she made vacant when she stood up to model the sweater.

"Where you wanna go eat at?" she asked smiling ear to ear.

"Rocky Mount. Maybe go to Shoney's or try out a nice restaurant you might see while we out there," K.B. suggested.

"What time you gon' close up? Do we have time for me to go home and change?" Gloria asked, putting the sweater back in the blue Belk's shopping bag.

There was a commotion going on in the barbershop that interrupted K.B. and Gloria and it sounded like screaming and yelling. K.B. and Gloria rushed out of the office.

"…you must be mad because I neva gave you the chance when you tried so hard when we were in high school." Patricia was screaming at Jerome.

"Ay, yo! What's goin' on out here?" K.B. interrupted. Everyone got quiet when they heard his voice.

Patricia was heated and turned to look at K.B. but when she saw Gloria her anger was increased and she rolled her eyes. Then she went back to putting her items away in her cabinet.

"Yo, Rome, what's the problem, fam?" K.B. asked directly. Jerome was hesitant to answer.

"Yea, Jerome, tell him what the problem is?" Patricia taunted.

K.B. turned to Pat and she averted his gaze. Gloria rolled her eyes wating for her chance to put her two cents into the altercation.

"There ain't no problem, boss man. We just having a friendly disagreement on something and Pat got a li'l upset," Jerome said.

"Shit, with all that cackling she was doin', I know she was more than just upset," Gloria interjected.

Patricia stared daggers at Gloria then turned her back and poked her robust ass out as she bent down to finish straightening up her cabinet.

"Aight, well y'all cut it out. I don't want none of that shit goin' down in here. This is a place of business, not gossip," K.B. responded.

"I hear ya, boss man; it won't happen like that again," Jerome said, offering an apology.

"Thank you for coming out here and puttin' an end to all these accusations Keith," Patricia said, batting her eyes at K.B.

Gloria caught on to Pat calling K.B. by his government name and became infuriated.

"Don't feel special 'cause we didn't come out here to defend you, honey. We only came out here to stop that crazy cackling noise you was making," Gloria said with contempt.

Everyone in the barbershop stared at Gloria then at Patricia. From the way things were starting to play out, it seemed like Gloria suspected Patricia was fucking K.B. and was pissed off.

K.B. could tell by all the wide-eyed looks that shit was getting out of hand and he didn't want it to escalate.

"Come on, ma, don't feed into this bullshit and keep it going. Let's dead it from here," K.B. spoke to his woman.

"Hol' on. I didn't get a chance to respond," Patricia stated, looking at Gloria and ignoring K.B.'s stare. "Gloria, can you please tell me what I've done to you to make you not like me? It seems that you sincerely have an issue with me and I think we need to get to the bottom of it tonight," Patricia blurted out.

That was all Gloria needed from her to go off. "I just don't like you! Does that answer your fuckin' question?" Gloria was rolling her eyes and preparing to pounce on Patricia with the quickness. K.B. gripped her forearm tightly to restrain her before she impulsely sprung into action.

"No, it doesn't answer my question. Can I just take a guess? Can it be because I'm really cute and young and you might be just a tad bit jealous of me?" Patricia said in her sweetest voice. "Or could it be something else?" She looked over at K.B.

Gloria struggled with K.B., trying to get free to grab Patricia, but his hold was too tight.

"Let me go K! Let me go so I can stomp a mud hole in this country bitch!" Gloria screamed while all the customers and barbers looked on in shock.

"Please let her go K.B. so I can give her a good ole' country beat-down. Listen here gurl, please don't think that becuz I'm quiet, respectful, and from the South that I can't scrap. I will step outside of myself and kick your city tail all over this here barbershop and still speak to you after as if I never skull dragged you 'round this shop!" Patricia boomed, putting her hair in a ponytail.

Everyone was anxious to see something jump off between the Brooklyn girl and their high school homecoming queen. Gloria wiggled free from K.B.'s grip and charged at Patricia like a panther, her arms stretched out in front of her. Patricia stood her ground, her left leg extended behind her in preparation for the collision. She timed Gloria's moves perfectly and lowered her head as Gloria slammed into her. Patricia's head met Gloria's midsection with so much force that Gloria bounced back like a rag doll, falling backward into the cabinets, thoroughly winded. Patricia rushed over to her with the agility and speed of a cat and threw four explosive blows to her gut as the remaining air in Gloria's lungs escaped through sickening "UMPH" noises. Patricia continued raining heavy blows on Gloria, not giving her the chance to catch her breath. Gloria tried to cover up in vain as Patricia viciously kicked her in her side until she scurried into a corner. Then she grabbed Gloria by the ankles and yanked her back to her, Patricia then bent down and continued pounding her fists into Gloria's face. No one in the barbershop attempted to grab Patricia except K.B., who pulled her away from his girlfriend effortlessly. Then he grabbed Gloria and pulled her to her feet.

Gloria was winded and sounded as if she was having an asthma attack. Patricia regrouped and charged at her again, swinging wildly over K.B.'s back. He maneuvered so her blows would only reach him. He turned around and grabbed her by the arm and shoved her into her barber's chair then shuffled Gloria to the back office.

"Damn, you fucked her up with the quickness," Jerome said to a heavily breathing Patricia in a hushed tone when K.B. disappeared through the office doors.

Patricia turned and looked at him and smiled a devilish grin: "I told her we scrap in the South."

Although they just had an argument, repping the South was Patricia and Jerome's foremost focus when an outsider violated. The rest of the patrons in the barbershop nodded their heads in agreement. This was the South and New Yorkers had a tendency to think that they were better and smarter than the country folk, so they stuck together in the face of any adversity. Patricia just showed what the country was made of.

"I'm gonna fuck that simple bitch up!" Gloria screamed to K.B. after recovering from the quick ass whipping she received.

"Chill, ma. That shit shoulda never happened," K.B. said, attempting to calm her down.

"Nah, that shit was supposed to happen. That bitch act like she the shit in this shop. She don't get no special treatment 'cause she the only girl that work in here. She just like the rest of the barbers in here, K! She don't get no special fucking treatment." Gloria yelled loud enough for everyone in the shop to hear.

"Who said she was?" K.B. asked.

"It's not who says she is, it's how you treat the bitch, K. I be seeing how you look at her; I got eyes. I don't want that bitch working here no more," Gloria told him.

"Wait a minute, ma. We running a business here and her monthly rent helps pay the bills so let's not rush to get her up out of here so fast. You speaking personally, but we have to keep this business-related," K.B. reasoned.

"Her li'l bit of monthly rent ain't carrying this barbershop, K. I do the books, I know the expenses and her part don't really fucking matter. And if it did, we can

replace the bitch. She not the only bitch in North Carolina that know how to braid fucking hair!" Gloria was fuming.

K.B. could see it was futile to try and reason with Gloria because she was heated. He needed to get her away from the shop and continue with his plans to take her out to eat. Then he could show her the new house to take her mind off the events that just happened.

"Come on, Glo', let's just get outta here like we planned. Don't let this shit stop what we was gon' do," K.B. said, smoothing out her hair.

Gloria looked up at K.B. with accusing eyes—like he fucked Patricia. He was so quick to come to her defense about leaving the shop. She just lost the fight and couldn't stand to face Patricia every day knowing a country girl, who seemed to have her man on her side, defeated her. Before it was all said and done, Patricia would not be working in that shop, even if she had to threaten to leave K.B. for it to happen.

Chapter 13
****Shondra****

The weatherman on the news report said there would be showers and thunderstorms with periods of torrential downpours. The weather had been brutal in Brooklyn since spring threatened to come early. The winter holidays passed rather quickly and a new year rang in with no real promise of change. Everyone seemed to be getting back into their daily routine after enjoying the joys of Christmas and New Year's; the reality of life was abundantly clear when the bills arrived in the mail reminding them the party was over. Life seemed so unfair at this juncture, it was unpredictable and a challenge for those faced with problems on a scale so large, it was almost impossible to deal with on their own. No one could relate more than Shondra. She was in a very bad situation and was alone to make the decision of a lifetime.

Chico had finally made it official with her after months of procrastinating. Now they were a couple and there was no hiding or disrespect on her part, or on his. Their relationship was growing slowly and there were issues they faced that could be worked out easily with

time. Shondra had neither spoken to nor seen Junior since the night they made love in the hotel and he left on the run. During that time she wasn't sure if she would ever speak to him if he came back, but since he made no attempts to contact her she was sure it was over between them. It devastated her that their relationship dissolved the way it did. But Chico's presence seemed to fill the void of Junior's absence in its own way and she was thankful to him for that. Nonetheless, getting over Junior was not easy; deep inside she longed to see him again. She put her head down and searched for a tissue in her Louie tote bag to wipe away the tears that were about to make an appearance from the overwhelming thoughts of Junior her mind would not let her soon forget.

"You OK, sweety?" A gray haired elderly woman with a walker asked.

"I'm…I'm OK, ma'am," Shondra responded, wiping her tears away.

"Whatever it is, chile, let go and let God," she said, passing Shondra a Jehovah's Witness pamphlet she readily had in her hand to pass out to anyone who would take it.

Shondra took the pamphlet and held onto it and read the bold letters on the front, "Life or Death Is Coming: Are You Ready?" Shondra cried even more and shook her head. It was too much for her to bear.

"Ms. Haynes? Ms. Haynes?"

Shondra heard her last name and stood up and walked out the door without responding. She headed down the stairs almost tripping and falling from her hurried, unbalanced steps. When she reached the exit door to the outside world, she bumped into people coming into the entrance as she tried to get out. She stopped at the bottom of the stairs to catch her breath. The tears were flowing

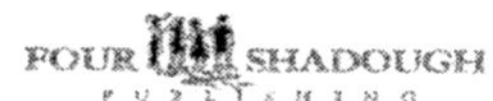

uncontrollably from her eyes as she held the banister for support and succumbed to the wealth of emotions she was feeling. A young fair-skinned girl approached Shondra seeing she was clearly in distress then stopped and looked at her for a couple of seconds.

" 'Scuse me. Why are you crying? Did you change your mind or are you sorry you did it?" she asked, moving closer to Shondra.

Shondra looked up at her sobbing and realized the young girl was most probably facing a situation similar to her own.

"I had a change of heart. I don't have the right to take a life," Shondra cried. "Regardless of what anyone will say or think, my baby has the right to life."

The young girl's eyes became misty and just like Shondra needed a wake up call, she too needed to hear something that allowed her to make a conscious decision without the pressure of outside sources. Shondra dug into her bag and gave her the same pamphlet the gray-haired old woman had given her. She thanked Shondra and turned quickly on her heels and headed away from the abortion clinic. Shondra rubbed her stomach and continued her journey back to Baptiste knowing the decision she just made was going to change the course of her life forever.

****Junior****

Junior maneuvered the all-black Jeep Cherokee Limited into the parking lot of the Tompkins project houses. Craig was in his usual spot in the parking lot surrounded by his workers and some females from the area. Everyone turned their heads when they saw the Jeep enter the parking lot; no one knew Junior was driving the

shiny black Cherokee with gold BBS rims and tinted windows. Some of Craig's boys moved out the way of the approaching vehicle, grabbing their guns and holding it down to their side just in case whoever was driving had plans of an ambush.

"What's up, cuz?" Junior yelled, jumping out of the driver's side of the Jeep.

"What's good, man?" Craig said when he saw his young cousin was the driver.

Junior was donning a thick, blue velour Fila sweatsuit with a pair of crispy white Filas. He had gotten two gold fronts and upgraded his chain to an 18" cable rope chain with a house piece along with a solid gold watch. Craig hadn't seen Junior since he repaid him the money he lent him to get back on his feet. Judging from the way things were looking, Junior was doing better than when he was when he was slinging in Baptiste. His energy and confidence was refreshing but seemed to have an arrogant air to it.

"I see you, baby cuz. I see you shining. That's a nice Jeep you pushing. What's the damage?" Craig asked, looking at the rims.

"I'm getting mad paper down there, cuzzo. It's so sweet; I'm the man down that piece already. Oh, and the Jeep was a light seventeen thou, nothing crazy," Junior said, inspecting the girls looking at his new Jeep.

"A light seventeen thou, huh? It's in your name?" Craig asked.

"Nah, cuz, I put that in shorty name. I ain't trying to put nothing in my name. I ain't playin' no games, cuzzo, shorty got North Carolina license and the whole nine. You think I wasn't paying attention when you used to talk to

me. I told you I was gon' turn it up when I got down there," Junior explained proudly.

"I see you doing what you supposed to be doing. How much paper you bringing in?" Craig asked being nosy.

"I be doin' like eighty to ninety gees. That money liquid, ya feel me? Flows just like agua," Junior chuckled.

"Damn kid, you doing some big numbers," Craig said, looking at Junior suspiciously.

"That's not the half. On some real shit, I just counted out about forty from the three days I been down there. I'm here 'cause I had to bring Muff to see her moms 'cause she slipped on the job and hurt her back. I still got like two keys down there working. I know when I get back down there it's gon' be close to finished so before I go back I'ma cop another two keys."

"They buying your shit up like that? You doing hand to hand or you got some workers other than cousin Bo?" Craig asked.

"That's that butter I'm spreading down there and I don't have no workers except for Bo and I'm not doing hand to hand. That's the sweet part about it, I'm selling weight to them country boys the same way you supplying the cats out here," Junior explained.

Craig was impressed with Junior. He looked at his young cousin and began to envy him. His determination paid off for him and his idea to go out of town was one he now wished he had partnered in instead of just lending Junior the money to get started.

"You still fucking with Venezuelo?" Craig asked Junior.

"Nah, I found another connect and his shit is Parkay. Plus, he givin' up crazy low prices per gram."

“Word? Why you ain’t put me on to him if it’s like that?” Craig asked in wonderment.

“I know the kind of relationship you got wit’ Venezuelo, so I didn’t think you would want to change that,” Junior answered.

“Yea, but you didn’t even ask. If I can get more bang for my buck, why wouldn’t I change? Its just business at the end of the day, that muhfucka would either match it or let me go. So you moving some heavy weight out there huh, li'l cuz?” Craig eyed the brick print in Junior’s sweats.

“I’m doing my thing. They showin’ me mad love, too. And the bitches, yo, them country bitches is thick as fuck, Craig, and they like to fuck crazy.”

Junior talked with Craig and caught up on things that were going on while he was away in North Carolina. As they spoke, Craig asked him something that brought back old feelings.

“What’s up with you and Shondra? When the last time you seen or spoke to her?” Craig asked.

The question blew Junior back because since he’d been down south, he hadn’t heard from Shondra. He hadn’t he tried to contact her either. Just hearing her name made his heart skip a beat and bring forward the feelings he tried to suppress long before leaving to go to North Carolina.

“Ain’t nothing up between us. Last time we spoke was when I first left. I don’t know what’s up with her but I probably do need to go check on her,” Junior said.

“You need to find out if they still looking for you over there in Baptiste,” Craig warned.

“I’m sure they are but I don’t give a fuck. They not gon’ catch me over there lunchin’, trust me, cuz. I’m not

letting the boys in blue stop what I'm doin'. Ya feel me?" Junior said with confidence.

"I hear you talking. All I'm saying is be careful and watch your back if you plan on going through there. What's up with that Puerto Rican dude that owed you that bread? Did you ever straighten that out?" Craig asked.

"No question. I licked at that muhfucka one day when I went to pick up my money. Oh shit, I forgot to tell you about that! I did that before I came to you for that start-up bread. Yo, you know that dude La is still alive?" Junior told him.

"Word? I remember that young boy. I remember telling you not to trust that muhfucka and he wound up trying to set you up. How he alive? I thought you said he got murked when that other cat got his wig pushed back?" Craig questioned.

"That's what I thought, too, cuz. That's what Rock—God bless the dead—told me when I asked him. So much happened between us I forgot to tell you I went around there with my shorty, Muff, to fuck Chico's ass up. While we was riding, I saw that same black Max with the back windows blown out. I knew it was the same car we tore the windows out of that night at the diner. I thought it was that dude K.B.'s whip at first but I found out it was La's because he tried to ambush me after that faggot-ass Chico ran in the building," Junior explained.

"You gon' have to take care of that dude fo' real, fam. That kind of beef you don't want hanging over your head," Craig said.

"I know it. While I'm checking on Shondra I'm gonna see if she can find out anything. If he out there in Baptiste she should know something and clue me in if she can," Junior said, walking over to his Jeep.

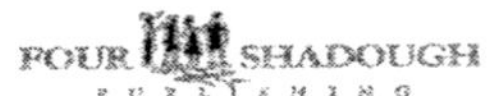

"When you goin' over there? You need some iron?" Craig asked.

"Nah, I'm strapped. I'm 'bout to shoot over there soon as I leave from over here," Junior said.

"Aight, cuz just be careful. And if you need me, just holla front," Craig let Junior know.

Junior slapped his cousin five and departed from Tompkins Houses.

La

La was rocking back and forth on the gate, waiting for the worker to pay him the rest of his money. Chico usually picked up but told La he had to go to Philly to visit his sick grandmother. La didn't believe his story and he didn't trust Chico ever since he busted him in a lie. That was the day Smiley was shot. Since La didn't have anybody he half-trusted, he had to take care of it himself. One thing Chico's absence taught him was that he needed to have a backup worker he could trust, just in case something ever happened to Chico. He definitely was out of pocket for picking up money and he was the boss.

The worker left to make a sale then he was supposed to go to his stash and get the rest of the count. La was in the back of the building watching the steady flow of traffic coming and going, mentally counting how much money was coming through the building. He walked to the side of the building and noticed a dark-colored vehicle parked directly across the street from the building attempting to look inconspicuous among the rest of the parked cars. He retraced his steps walking backward then went around the back of the building to get a better vantage point to be sure that whoever was in the car was watching

him. He hurried to the other side, peeked around the corner of the building and saw the two Caucasian occupants, confirming his suspicions.

"Slick muhfuckas! I'm glad I came through the back of the building and spotted them before they made a move," he thought to himself. "Well they not goin' to get the big fish today."

La walked back to the building and ran up the stairs, heading to the worker's house but bumped into him on his way up.

"Yo, po po outside; if you dirty get clean now!" La told him.

"Where they at?" The worker asked.

La shoved the worker hard and he fell backward onto the stairs. "Just go get clean, muhfucka. Don't worry 'bout where the fuck they at!"

"Aight, man," he said, running up the stairs to his house to put away the money and drugs he had on him.

La turned and walked back down the stairs and out the back of the building. His car was parked on Graham Avenue. Luckily he left his gun inside before coming to the building so he was clean except for a couple hundred dollars he had in small bills in his pocket. As he walked through the parking lot toward his car was, he felt a strong tug on his arm. Immediately, he went into defense mode and started swinging wildly. Someone grabbed his other arm and he was taken down hard to the concrete.

"What the fuck is your problem, boy? Don't you know it's a felony to assault a police officer?" Taylor said to La, his knee in his back.

"What you want, man?" La moaned, trying to wiggle free.

“What I want? You don’t remember me?” Taylor inquired, pulling La to his feet.

La immediately remembered the Caucasian detective from the intense interrogation while he was in the hospital recovering from his gunshot wound.

“I don’t remember you, Officer. Can you tell me where I know you from or why I would know you?” La changed his attitude.

Taylor looked at La suspiciously. When he and Burke tried to interrogate him in the hospital, he was a little delirious and in pain. It could be possible that he genuinely didn’t remember him. Taylor took the safe approach. He brushed La off and stood back from him and began: “I’m the detective that has been assigned to your case. When you were in the hospital, I interviewed you to try and find out if you knew who shot you and left you to die in the back of 146 Humboldt Street. You were pretty bad off in there and almost didn’t make it. Me and my partner, Burke, over here,” pointing to Burke who was standing next to him, “we were in the hospital everyday hoping you would pull through so we could bring the perpetrator of this heinous crime to justice. Then one day we came to the hospital to get your statement and it was like you just disappeared into thin air. We couldn’t get a forwarding address or anything.”

“I’m sorry, Officer. I really can’t remember you,” La said, wearing a perplexed look.

“That’s OK. We can take your statement now and hopefully get the bastard that did that to you.” Taylor pulled out a small handheld note pad and flipped it open to a clean page in preparation to write down some information. “Now tell me, do you remember what

happened the day you were shot? Can you recall who shot you?" Taylor asked La, trying to read his expression.

La had no intention on giving them any information; he wasn't a snitch and wanted to get Junior himself without any help from the police.

"The only thing I remember is seeing this guy named Rock right before I got shot. Then everything went dark. I can't really remember anything else past that," La uttered, knowing full well who did the deed. He kept a distant look in his eyes as if he were trying to concentrate really hard.

"Are you saying Rock is the one that shot you? Can you think of a reason he would want to harm you?" Taylor asked with a raised eyebrow.

"I can't really say. All I remember was that I came in the building and he asked me for the time and when I looked down at my watch then looked back up to tell him, there was a gun in my face. Then I heard a loud boom and saw a flash of light. After that…nothing," La said with a straight face.

Taylor looked at Burke and then at La.

"You do know that Rock was killed some months ago, don't you?" Taylor asked.

"Yea, I actually saw that on the news. That's fucked up," La responded.

"Hmmm. You and he, were you guys friends?" Taylor asked.

"I wouldn't say he was a friend like that, but I knew him: we spoke, said what's up and all. That's really the extent of it." La rubbed his chest wound and balled his face up as if he were in pain.

“The day you were shot, do you recall seeing anyone else in the building or outside apart from Rock?” Taylor continued with his questions.

“Nope, I ain’t see nobody else out there that day; just Rock. Why?” La inquired.

“There was a young man who got killed the same day you were shot.” Taylor pulled out a mugshot of Drez and quickly shoved it in La’s face then studied his facial expression for a reaction.

“I never saw that guy before. I did hear that somebody got killed the same day I was shot. And now that I think about it, I’m really lucky to be alive,” La said, bowing his head and forcing crocodile tears for effect.

“Yea, you are the lucky one. Do you know a guy around here named Junior?” Taylor pushed further.

“Yea, I know him but just in passing. I ain’t seen him around since I came out of the hospital. I don’t really come out that much anymore,” La replied.

“Well, we’re not going to hold you up any longer. Here, take this card and if you can remember anything, just give me a call.

“By the way, how’s your recovery coming along?” Taylor asked, handing his police business card to La.

“I’m doing better, still feel a li'l stiff but I’m getting stronger as the days go by,” La replied, rubbing his chest and faking a defeated, painful expression. “It bothers me the most when it rains for some reason.”

“Glad to hear you’re doing better. Hope your health continues to improve. And if you remember anything, anything at all, just give me a call,” Taylor said as he and Burke turned to leave.

“OK, thanks, Officer. I will call if I remember anything,” La said in a cordial tone.

As the two detectives walked away Taylor turned his head and watched La walk up the block and disappear around the corner.

"Come on, partner." Taylor jogged to their unmarked car.

"Do you believe the bullshit he was shoveling?" Burke said, trying to keep pace with his partner.

"I was trying hard not to slap the fucking cuffs on his black ass. These monkeys think they're so smart. Now don't get me wrong: our informant could be giving us false information, but he seems more credible than that lying piece of shit we were just talking to. Could you believe the 'Yes, Officer, no, Officer,' 'I'm lucky to be alive, Officer' bullshit he was talking?" Taylor laughed, truly tickled by La's show of phony respect for him.

Taylor put the key in the ignition and the engine roared to life. Then he pulled out of his parking space and drove in the direction of La.

"The informant definitely knew what he was talking about. He said today we would be able to catch him in this building. I saw he ID'd us when he came out the building and figured he went and got clean when he came back out; that's why I decided not to search him to throw him off track. He thought he was pulling the wool over our eyes but once we tail him and find out some more information on him, we can take him down and then have him help us blow these murder cases wide open!"

****Shondra****

"Where you been?" Chico asked Shondra.

Shondra hadn't told Chico she was pregnant because she wasn't sure what his reaction would be. And he wasn't

aware that she went to the abortion clinic that morning. She could tell he was a little suspicious of her because he'd been keeping a close watch on her lately. He'd been staying in the house with her and hadn't been out of the house to hustle or for any trips to the store in almost a week.

"I thought I told you I was going downtown this morning," she answered.

"Oh, that's right; I forgot. What you went down there to get?" Chico questioned, looking at her empty hands for shopping bags.

"I went to look at some shoes but wound up looking at some outfits, too," Shondra replied.

"So, why you ain't buy nothing? All that money I gave you last night wasn't enough for what you wanted?" he asked her.

"No, Chico, what you gave me was more than enough. I was just down there basically looking at some shoes and outfits—you know my birthday is in a couple of months. I had a lot to choose from, so I just walked around and window-shopped before making a decision on buying anything. You still ain't been outside?" she asked, noticing he still was in his boxers.

"Nah, I told you: I'm on a vacation. I'm taking a break because it's been hot out there lately," Chico told her.

"OK, I was just asking. Do you want something from the store before I take my clothes off and get settled?" she asked him, going to her closet to change her pocketbook.

"Yea, I feel like eating something from the Spanish restaurant on Manhattan Avenue. Can you go there and get me the stewed chicken with red beans and plantains? Oh,

and pick up some blunts, too." Chico produced some crumpled-up bills from his front pockets and peeled some off and gave them to Shondra.

Chico's sloppy and unorganized finances irritated Shondra; he never knew how much money he had in his pockets because he kept it balled up. That's how she was able to get the money she was going to use for the abortion.

She took the money he gave her for his food and left the house. When she exited the building, she sighed heavily because Chico's immaturity sometimes showed through in his childish way of doing things. She had to wonder if he would be a good father to her unborn child. There were a lot of things she had to think about before even telling him she was with child and time was not on her side. She continued up Siegel Street to the restaurant, her thoughts on having the baby and actually breaking the news to Chico flooded her mind. She mindlessly walked into the street not watching the flow of traffic and heard the screeching of tires and jumped back on the curb just as the vehicle skidded past her. The driver backed up and stopped at the curb right next to her. Shondra was prepared to apologize to the driver because she wasn't paying attention. The passenger window rolled down and her heart dropped when she saw the driver.

"What's up, Mooka?" Junior said, his eyes fixed on her facial expression.

Shondra was at a loss for words and couldn't respond.

"Get in. I want to talk to you. You know I'm not supposed to be over here," Junior said, waving her inside the Jeep.

Shondra heard the automatic locks and quickly grabbed the door handle and entered the Jeep not knowing

what Junior wanted to talk to her about. She was half-hoping it was to reconcile their differences. Once inside the Jeep, Junior rolled up the tinted windows and slowly pulled off. He turned to Shondra and looked at her briefly as he cruised down Graham Avenue. She was looking a little unkempt, her fingernails needed to be done, her weave was showing the new growth, her complexion seemed more bland than he remembered, and she had dark circles under her eyes like she hadn't had a good, peaceful sleep in months. Her clothing was also not what he was used to seeing her wear: they were more baggy than usual.

"Are you OK, Shondra?" he asked with concern. It came across sounding more like pity.

Shondra was embarrassed when she heard the tone in Junior's voice. It had been months since she saw him and he seemed to be brimming with more confidence than she ever remembered. He was still dressed as sharply as ever: he still had his hair cut in a low Caesar with the waves spinning, his complexion was bright and still bubbly, and his voice was strong with a tad bit more bass. Junior still looked good to her and she looked like a peasant compared to what she used to look like.

"I'm OK, Junior. How you been? I haven't heard from you since the last time we saw each other in the hotel. I'm guessing you been down south?" she asked.

"Yea, I been down there doin' exactly what I said I was gonna do, baby. I came through to see if me and you can get some things straight since the last time we talked."

"Junior, please don't do this to me. You know you don't want me and I know when you left you took that deranged bitch down there with you. You lied to me," Shondra blurted out.

"Ah, come on, Shondra; don't start that shit again. I thought we was past that bullshit. I'm done with the bitch. She ain't around me like that anymore," Junior replied bluntly.

"You right. Well what happened to you coming back and me and you starting over? Huh? What happened to that?" Shondra's emotions were taking over. "You think I'm real stupid, huh, Junior? You think that because I love you that I'm blind to your bullshit? I believed you when you said you wanted to save our relationship. I believed you when you said you wanted to change, but that night we spent together you was lying out those gold fronts. I know you spoke to that bitch, Muffin, and I know you was taking her down there instead of me." Shondra's chest was heaving. "And to think I believed you! I thought you was sincere and the whole time you was bullshitting me! How could you do me like that, Junior? How could you choose her over me?" She silently cursed herself for not being able to hold back the tears that were impossible to stop from flowing.

Junior pulled over and put the Jeep in park then turned to face her. "You know what? Fuck it. I'm gonna keep it real for a fucking change. Ain't no need to keep bullshitting you. It's been a long time and you're right, I was seeing Muffin. I slept with her and the whole shit but I don't love her, Mooka. I love you. I admit I fucked up and I'm sorry. I want us to try to be together again, seriously. Too much was happening before but I'm in better position to make decisions without worrying about the repercussions. All I need from you is patience. I need you to trust me again and believe from here on in I'm going to tell you the truth."

Shondra wanted to believe him but her heart was telling her to retreat and leave well enough alone. Junior wasn't going to change and she was mentally fucked up when it came to him because seeing him threw her emotions in disarray. She couldn't control herself and no matter how bad he treated her, she was still deeply in love with him. To be fooled and hurt by the same man over and over again would make it seem she was a glutton for punishment and she needed to be strong so she would not continue to be a fool to her love for him.

She was in a world of confusion. If she told him she wasn't willing to try again it would most likely be the last time she would ever see him again but if she told him she was willing to give it another try then she would be betraying the relationship she formed with Chico. She had promised she wouldn't leave him if Junior ever came back into the picture. She looked at Junior and his eyes were still mystical to her. She yearned for those early years in their relationship where she never questioned his love for her. She was preparing to tell him of the decision she was going to make and suddenly she heard, "Yo, get out!"

Junior screamed the words to her and jerked his Jeep in drive while holding his foot on the brake pedal.

"What's wrong, Junior? What happened?" Shondra screamed, pulling the handle on the door and exiting the Jeep looking around nervously.

"Close the door!" Junior screamed not looking at her.

Shondra slammed the door shut and Junior pulled off from the curb, leaving her standing on the sidewalk inhaling the asphalt that kicked up from his screaming tires.

La

La turned the corner and quickly walked to his car that was parked on the corner of Graham Avenue. He looked back once before he jumped into the driver's side to make sure the detectives weren't following him. To La, it wasn't a coincidence the detectives just happened to be in Baptiste and randomly rolled up on him: someone had given them some detailed information on him. He put the key in the ignition and was about to turn the key to start the engine when he caught a glimpse of movement in his peripheral vision. He saw a vehicle approaching on the corner and he quickly slumped down in his seat to avoid detection. He peeked up momentarily to see if he was spotted by the detectives. After the vehicle turned the corner, he started his car and pulled out the parking space he was in and headed out of Baptiste.

Junior couldn't botch the opportunity that just presented itself. Although seeing Shondra again after so long ignited his feelings, seeing La drive by held more importance. Squashing his beef with La took precedence over seeing Shondra and discussing their relationship. The situation was perfect because he had the drop on him and that gave him full autonomy to handle it anyway he saw fit. He didn't have a strategic plan in place because he didn't expect to see La; he was going to play it by ear. If he were given a clear shot of him with an exit and no witnesses, he was going to take it. If not, he was just going to follow him until an opportunity presented itself.

Junior followed the Maxima turning left on Washington Avenue and then right on Fulton Street. La seemed to be heading toward downtown Brooklyn. The Maxima suddenly pulled over abruptly and La jumped out

the vehicle and followed behind a young woman with a sexy body. He pulled over so quickly that Junior had to pass the Nissan and pull over a couple cars ahead. He watched La in his rearview mirror as he made advances on the young lady he was talking with. Then he witnessed them exchanging numbers. La jumped back into his vehicle and resumed down Fulton Street. Junior waited for him to pass by him then looked at the young lady walking up the block. He rolled down his passenger window when she came past his Jeep then pulled out a wad of money.

"Ay, shorty. Yo, li'l mama," he yelled to her through the open window.

She turned toward Junior and when she saw the shiny Jeep Cherokee, she immediately walked over and put her head inside the passenger window.

"Yea, hun. You want something?" she replied in a sultry voice.

"Listen, ma, I don't have a lot of time to talk but I need that number that scrams just gave you," Junior said quickly.

"For what?" she asked suspiciously.

"I just need it, baby. How much is it worth to you?" Junior peeled off some bills from the stack he had in his hand.

The young lady's eyes grew wide at the amount of money Junior was holding in his hands. Her gold-digger radar went up immediately and she went into black widow mode.

"I'll give it to you no problem hun. But can I get yours in return?" She eyed Junior hungrily.

Junior laughed at her trying to mack him but that didn't deter from the task at hand. "Here, baby. This is five hundred. Just write your math down on this paper" Junior

handed her a napkin from his console while watching to see if he still had La's car in sight.

She wrote her number down and gave him both numbers. Then she said, "You better call me too, handsome."

Junior smiled and drove away, hoping La didn't get too far. He stepped on the gas, accelerating quickly then slowed down as he went through intersections to see if he could spot the Maxima. He was about to give up when he saw a black car up ahead of him about two blocks away. He sped up and passed through a red light so he wouldn't lose his target again. He slowed down when he got directly behind the black car and continued to follow him.

La was on his way to one of his girls' houses in Crown Heights on St. Marks Avenue. He was going to shack up there for a minute. He needed to stay away from Baptiste for a little while since the detectives seemed to be hot on his trail. He couldn't shake the idea that Chico conveniently happened to be visiting his sick grandmother while detectives showed up at his spot to talk to him. He couldn't prove it, but he was going to find out. Once he did, he was going to get rid of him because he wasn't about to let anyone or anything become a hindrance to his operation.

When La was in front of his girl's house, he got out of his vehicle and walked to a telephone booth on the corner. He deposited a quarter and dialed her number to make sure she was home. While he waited for someone to pick up on the other line, he turned around and noticed a black Jeep Cherokee parked on the corner across from where he was standing. The gold rims made it stick out like a sore thumb. Unlike the truck, he was trying to avoid standing out. He tried to see who was driving the truck, almost sure it was a hustler sitting on something so pretty. As much as he liked how the truck looked, he couldn't get anything that loud because the heat was on him and to be seen in something fancy would be detrimental to the flow of his money at this point; he still admired it. He continued to peer through the tints and could swear the silhouette of the guy driving looked strangely familiar. His thoughts were interrupted when the person on the other line answered.

"Hello?" the sweet, sexy voice said.

"What's up, baby? What you doin'?" La asked.

"Nothing, La. What's up with you? I thought you was going to come over last night? What happened?" the girl asked.

"I got caught up last night, baby. I had to handle some business that couldn't be put on hold," he responded.

"There you go with your excuses. I cooked and everything for you and you stood me up once again," she said.

"I didn't mean to and I'll make it up to you. I'm outside on the payphone on the corner. I'm coming to the crib 'cause I need to talk to you about making some new arrangements and hopefully you'll be wit' it," La explained, peeking at the Jeep periodically.

"You right outside? Why you ain't just come to the house, boy?" she asked.

"You know I don't move like that. I gotta call before I come; don't wanna catch no shit I ain't 'posed to see. You feel me?" La chuckled.

"I don't see how 'cause you calling from right down the block; you would see everything. Stop your bullshit and come here, boy," she said.

"Aight, I'll be there in a minute.' La hung up the phone and walked to the building and rang the intercom. Then he waited to get buzzed in. Before he entered, he took one more look at the Jeep that was still parked on the corner. Something was weird but he just couldn't put his finger on it.

Junior watched La enter the building and took note of the address and building number. The wheels were turning in his head and he figured the building was where one of La's many freaks lived. The area was quiet and it seemed like the perfect place to body him. He sat in his Jeep another couple of minutes and then left. He was determined to get La and he wasn't going to rest comfortably until he knew he was dead.

Chapter 14
****Shondra****

Shondra was on her way back home but was worried about what had just happened with Junior. When he pulled off she looked around but didn't see any signs of police or impending danger. She couldn't figure out what was so urgent.

Seeing him again raised a lot of confusing emotions and thoughts she was trying to put behind her. It was difficult to just forget or remove him completely from her life. There were days and nights when he preyed heavily on her mind and she would think about him so hard she would wake up calling his name. Chico was present one of those nights but she lied and told him she was having a nightmare that Junior was trying to hurt her. Chico's young mind accepted the lie and she kept her secret.

Chico did treat her rather sensibly and was trying to be a good dude but his youthful antics sometimes made her wonder if she moved too fast in getting into a serious relationship with him. The past few months being with Chico proved to be a job within itself. It was getting more and more complicated dealing with his ways and it was

taking a toll on her. Her health was now a major issue to worry about. A child was developing in her womb and that had to be the single most important thing to her, over Junior or Chico.

She made it to the building just as she was becoming sick. She hurriedly put the key in the lock and pushed her way into the house. She went into the kitchen and put all the bags on the counter and ran to the bathroom to purge. She was only six weeks along but was getting sick regularly. When she threw up it felt like her intestines were coming out of her mouth. When she was done, she wiped the sweat from her brow, rose to her feet, then flushed the toilet. She went to the sink and looked at herself and she looked a hot mess. She wondered what Junior really thought of her when he saw her and began to cry. She was upset with the direction her life was going; she was making some bad choices and now she was with child, which changed the game. She didn't have a job, any money, a place of her own, or any of the necessities needed to take care of another life. She couldn't wish on a star for everything to go right. She would have to become a good mother and make the best of her bad situation with Chico. She would just have to guide him into being a good father, and for the most part, she thought he did have some good qualities.

She walked out of the bathroom and went into the kitchen to get his food. She took the plastic lid off the round aluminum tray and placed a plastic fork inside the meal. She grabbed a Pepsi she bought for him to wash his food down and carried everything to her room. Her hands were full. She was about to knock on the bedroom door when she heard faint moans coming from inside her room.

She put her ear to the door and listened as moans of passion echoed.

She became sick all over again. There was no way Chico was that stupid or that disrespectful to bring another bitch into her crib, she thought. She was shaking with rage but decided to catch him on the downstroke. She quickly went back to the kitchen to get a steak knife just in case he felt froggish.

She walked quickly back to her room and put her ear to the door and she could hear him moaning and talking dirty to the bitch. She turned the knob on the door and slowly pushed it open. It took all the restraint she could muster to not just kick the door in and go to work on both their trifling asses. But she thought she could be more diplomatic; the element of surprise was on her side.

When the door opened, she witnessed Chico lying on the bed, back turned on the cordless phone. She walked over to the black lacquer nightstand and pressed the speaker button on the telephone base and Chico jumped when he heard the audible voice coming through the speakers. He turned around with his dick in his hand and had a look of shock mixed with embarrassment.

"Yea, you like that shit, huh, Chico? Stroke that dick for me. Yea, baby, make that shit cum for me. Tell me that's my dick, daddy. Tell Mimi that dick belong to her. Mmmm. Yes, daddy, I miss daddy dick in this pussy…" the seductive female voice serenaded through the speakers.

That was all Shondra could take hearing. Before Chico could put his dick back in his boxers, Shondra swung at his head with her free hand and busted his lip as he tried to block the blow.

"What the fuck you think you doin', muhfucka? You nasty fuck!" Shondra screamed, trying to connect again with her free hand.

"Hold up, Shondra," Chico stammered, trying to roll out of bed and get himself together.

Shondra jumped over the bed and dropped the steak knife as she swung wildly with both hands, hitting him as he crashed to the floor.

"Hold up? Are you fucking crazy? You having phone sex with a bitch in my fucking house? Did you lose your fucking mind for real?" Shondra was livid. She struck out for him again, but this time he had his footing together and grabbed her arms and pushed her forcibly onto the bed. He jumped on top of her and tried to restrain her so he could explain away the bullshit he got caught doing red-handed.

"Get the fuck off me, Chico, and get the fuck outta my crib. I don't want your disrespectful ass around me no more. Get the fuck out!" Shondra's anger released hot tears from her eyes.

"You not gon' let me explain what happened?" That was the best he could do to buy himself time to think of something he thought she would believe.

"Are you stupid for real, muhfucka? You think you can explain that shit to me? You must really think I'm a dumb bitch, huh, Chico? Would you get the fuck off me and get the fuck out? I don't need no explanation to what you was doin'. I saw it with my own two eyes and heard with my ears. You lucky I didn't stab you in your fucking heart, bitch!" Shondra struggled to get free from his hold but he was too strong.

"I just want to tell you how it went down. I was trying…" Chico started.

“Save it, muhfucka. I don’t wanna hear no lies. Just get the fuck off me and get outta my crib. You ain’t neva gotta worry ‘bout me saying nothing else to your dumb ass.” She kicked her legs furiously. “That’s my word. I’m done. You so foul to do some shit like that after I done told you what I already been through with Junior. Just get the fuck out!”

Chico loosened his hold on her and made his way off the bed. He quickly put on his sweatpants then grabbed his sneakers off the floor and his sweatshirt that was on the edge of the bed and walked toward the bedroom door. He was going to turn around when he reached the door to tell her that he was sorry but the pain from the hard clay ashtray replaced any words that were going to form in his mouth.

“And I thought you woulda been a good father,” Shondra said, looking for something else to throw at Chico.

What Shondra said didn’t register in Chico’s head because he was too busy trying to get the fuck out of her house before she threw something that would land him in the hospital. He couldn’t retaliate because he knew he was dead wrong. Chico ran to the door holding his head from the wound created by the ashtray and then left hearing something else crash against the front door as he made his exit.

“That bitch is crazy,” he said to himself, making his way to his house.

As he walked toward his building, he didn’t want anyone in the hood to see him. He walked on the outskirts of the Projects and made it to his building safely without anyone seeing him who would run back and tell La. He hurried into the building and said a prayer.

Chapter 15
****Shondra****

Six weeks passed and Shondra's stomach had grown larger. She was making her prenatal appointments faithfully and found out she was anemic. Her doctor told her she would need plenty of bed rest when she reached her third trimester. She was concerned because she wanted a healthy baby and didn't want to do anything to jeopardize her pregnancy. At times she could feel the fluttering of life in her womb and that brought a smile to her face. She was lonely emotionally but physically felt new life. Once she gave birth, she thought, she would never be alone again; she would be surrounded by unconditional love from her baby.

She went into the bathroom and turned the tub faucets on to prepare her a bath for the day. Since kicking Chico out of her house, he had been coming by and calling, trying to apologize and ask for another chance but she hadn't given in. She had been through enough bullshit with Junior to ever deal with another man's disrespectful ways. She couldn't believe he would even violate her the way he did, knowing what she had been through with Junior. Her luck with men was proving to be nothing short of bad choices. It was time for her to forget about having a man and concentrate on Shondra and that's what the birth of her child was going to allow her to do. Becoming a mother was the most important thing to her and everything else would have to take a backseat to that.

Her pregnancy was having a positive effect on her as far as being more responsible and making more conscious decisions. It had a lot to do with her being the sole protector of the life in her womb and knowing every decision she made would have a direct impact on her child.

She still hadn't spoken to Chico about her pregnancy. Even though she alluded to the fact when she kicked him out, for some reason he never said anything. She never said anymore about it to him. They were not together anymore, officially, so she didn't want to create any confusion by having him think she was having the baby because she wanted him back.

She didn't want him to think she was hard up for a father for her child because her intention was to take care of her child herself; however, she did want assistance from the father because one parent did not conceive the child. She didn't have any experience in raising a child but already knew what she wanted for her baby and was going to do everything in her power to ensure it's safe, healthy, and stable entry into the cruel and unforgiving world in which she lived.

***

Baptiste had been quiet since La wasn't putting much work out there. Chico was stuck with La and was broke after tricking all his money on Shondra. He needed

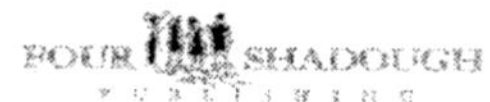

to make some money but it was hard because La was staying away from Baptiste until the heat died down. Chico was used to at least having a couple hundred dollars on him but was near broke because he didn't manage his money correctly. Without La, there was no money for him to maintain his small-time hustler lifestyle. He lost Shondra because he was reckless and the shorty he was fucking with left him as soon as his money ran out.

He walked to the phone booth and beeped La. He watched as a couple crackheads approached him but he quickly shook his head so they would know he wasn't working and didn't have anything. When the phone rang, Chico picked it up.

"Yo, who dis?" La asked, speaking in a dangerous tone.

"It's me, La: Chico. What's up, man? It's fucked up out here, man. When you gon' come through with some chicken?" Chico asked.

"When that snitching-ass muhfucka is dead!" La shot back.

"You ain't find out who it was yet?" Chico asked in a cautious tone.

"Nah, and until I find out which one of y'all rat ass muhfuckas is snitching, ain't nothing moving out there. And if a muhfucka try and get fast and put something out there and I find out, he might as well lay down when I see him. So let them clowns out there know that if they snitched on me because they wanna fry their own chicken to DX that idea." La said.

"Why you thinking it's one of the guys out here? Ain't none of them dudes gon' violate like that. They all making bread and I ain't never hear anybody complaining

about not being happy. It could be one of the people that live in the buildings or something," Chico suggested.

"Yea, aight. Whateva. Where you at right now?" La asked.

"I'm on Graham Avenue. What's up?" Chico asked, staring at a girl who walked by with tight spandex pants.

"If you want some chicken you can meet me and I'll hit you off. Aight?" La told him.

"OK; Where at?" Chico said eagerly.

"By Hylan Park, you know how to get out there?" La asked him.

"Yea, where you want me to meet you though? That park mad big," Chico told him.

"Just meet me at the gas station and we'll handle it from there," La said.

"Aight, cool," Chico responded.

"Meet me there like the next hour. The Exxon gas station right on Bushwick Avenue," La informed him.

"Aight, I'll be there. See you in an hour," Chico said, hanging up the payphone.

Chico went to Shondra's house to see if he could try to get through to her before going to meet La. He had developed strong feelings for her the time they were together and now that they weren't, he missed her. She did treat him better than any girl he was ever with and literally spoiled him. He had spoken with her but hadn't seen her since the day she kicked him out of her house.

He knocked on her door waiting for her to open it. When the door flew open, he looked down and was surprised.

"Yo, you pregnant?" he asked, his mouth gaping open.

"What you want, Chico?" Shondra asked ignoring his question. She could have kicked herself for opening the door looking the way she did.

"You pregnant, Shondra? Why you ain't tell me? You think I'm not gon' take care of my seed?" he asked, still looking at her stomach.

"Please, Chico. I don't want to talk about this right now. Did you want something?" she asked, trying hard to avoid his questions.

"I was coming over here to see if you calmed down yet so we could talk about getting back together…I mean, see if you would give me another chance," he said.

"Chico, I don't have time for you. I came to you and was straight up wit' you. I told you my situation and how I was feeling for you. I kept it real with you and gave you a chance—no, I gave us a chance. You proved you wasn't ready for a real relationship and maybe I pushed you into it now that I look back but I thought you were capable of handling a woman like me. I knew I did you wrong in the beginning but we started over new and all that happened before was supposed to be old news."

Shondra pulled her shirt down. "I can't deal with a young dude that ain't ready for what I have to offer as a woman. You violated in the worst way, you know how my last relationship went with Junior so you knew firsthand how I would feel about the shit you pulled in my crib. Anyway, I'm not mad anymore. We can be cool but won't be no late night knocks on the door or any other shit like that," Shondra clarified.

"Damn, Shondra, it was the first time. You act like I been doin' shit like that on the reg. I been true to you the whole time we been fucking with each other. I can see why

you got mad but you act like you caught me fucking. It was just phone sex," Chico reasoned.

"OK, Chico, it was just phone sex because the bitch wasn't here to fuck you in person. It was just over the phone now but you and her woulda fucked when you saw her if y'all wasn't already fucking behind my back. So save that shit for the toilet," Shondra said, rolling her eyes.

"I never fucked her and didn't have plans on fucking her," Chico confessed.

"I'm not an asshole, Chico. You had to call the bitch cause I know she don't have my number so please stop your shit, please," Shondra informed him.

"Aight, Shondra. I did call her but it was just to talk to her about something. But then she started talking nasty and shit and I kinda got sucked into it," Chico told her.

"I'ma leave this shit alone before you stick your foot deeper in your mouth. Tell me why you came over her again?" Shondra said, brushing him off.

"I told you I want us to try to get back together," Chico said.

"And I told you I'm not with your bullshit. You want me to believe you was only having phone sex, right? So, you saying if the bitch offered you the pussy you wouldn't take it, right?" Shondra quizzed him.

"Nah," he replied quickly.

"Cone on now. I don't know any guy that would turn down a shot of free pussy and you're no different and haven't done anything to prove otherwise. I just don't have the time nor energy to go through another heartbreak over a dirty muhfucka, Chico. You understand what I'm saying?" Shondra was drained.

"I do and I don't." Chico looked at her stomach." What's up with that?" he said pointing to her stomach.

"What's up with it?" she said sucking her teeth and rolling her neck.

"I'm saying. What we going to do 'bout that?" He was still pointing to her stomach.

Shondra looked down at her belly; it had grown round and was firm. Her navel stuck out in the tight t-shirt and her nipples mimicked her navel and showed its firmness through the fabric. She didn't want him to use her pregnancy as leverage for him to come back into her life but she was willing to allow him to accept he was about to be a father.

"I hope you do the right thing and take care of your responsibility, but that don't mean…"

Chico cut her off and held her stomach gently in his hands. She didn't resist as he rubbed it softly with one hand in a circle and looked at her lovingly.

"Boy or girl?" he asked softly.

"I don't know yet." For some reason Shondra was feeling a little emotional and welcomed Chico's heartfelt concern.

"I want a boy, a li'l Chico. Na mean?" He looked at Shondra.

"Mmm hmm," she answered while he continued rubbing her belly.

"We really need to talk, Chico." Shondra snapped back to her senses.

"'Bout what? I'm gon' take care of my seed. Matter of fact, I'm 'bout to go meet my man and get some work so I'ma have some bread to take care of my baby." He said to her proudly.

"That's not the only thing the baby gon' need, Chico. Do you plan to be in his or her life? Your money is good for providing but the baby is going to need both

parents. That means you need to grow up, Chico, or I'm not gonna want you 'round the baby. Do you understand what I'm saying?" Shondra said, rubbing her stomach.

"I hear you, Shondra. I want to be there for my seed. I want to be a good father," Chico said. Chico came from a broken home, so if he was to have a child, he wanted better than what he had in his own empty life.

"Chico, I'm serious. I don't want my child involved with a father that's not going to be around or locked up. My baby is going to need stability," Shondra said seriously.

"So let's get back together so we can raise him together," Chico suggested.

"We don't have to be together in order to raise the baby, Chico. All we have to do is have good communication when it comes to our child. You think you ready for this?" she asked.

"Do I have a choice?" he countered.

"I guess not. I was skeptical about telling you because I thought you would try and deny my child, but I see you're taking this serious. I'm surprised."

"That's what I'm tying to tell you. I know how to be a man, Shondra. I just need a chance to show you again."

"Hold on, let's just see what happens, alright, Chico?"

"I can respect that. When the baby 'posed to be born?"

"I'm due the second week of September. I'm in my second trimester," she told him.

"OK, does that give me time to get my shit together?" he asked.

"I guess, but it depends on what you talking 'bout, Chico. Don't disappoint your child by doing some dumb shit." She looked at him sternly.

"I'm not; I got this. You know if you have a boy or girl they gon' be light-skinned with good hair," he said, smiling.

"I'm not worried 'bout that, Chico. I just want the baby to be healthy," Shondra said, chuckling on the inside at how excited he was about her being pregnant. It was a good feeling for her and she hoped things would work out for her and her unborn child.

Chico got ready to head over to Hylan to pick up the work La had for him. He figured he would get back with Shondra after the baby was born. For the first time since he started hustling, he felt he had a purpose for what he was doing.

Chapter 15
******Muffin & Junior******

Muffin took off her clothes and prepared to take a shower. Junior came in late the night before and she didn't feel like bothering him with what she wanted to do this morning. Besides, he didn't like shopping with her anyway. She jumped in the shower and cleansed her body then quickly jumped out and pulled on some sweats and tied her head up in a Gucci scarf, picked up her monogrammed Gucci shoulder bag, and left the bedroom. She had about eighteen hundred dollars in her pocketbook, which was more than enough for what she was going to buy, and while she was out shopping she planned on picking up something for Junior. She always liked for him to look good.

As she hurried down the stairs, she passed her mother who was in the kitchen cooking, as usual.

"Good morning, ma," Muffin sang as she went to give her a kiss.

"Good morning, baby. Why you up so early? You usually sleep in late on the weekends," Ms. Turner said.

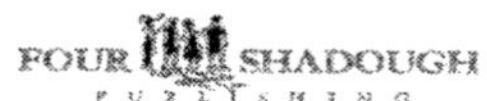

“I want to catch this sale they have in Bloomies, ma. You know we don’t pay full price for nothing if we can get it on sale.” Muffin smiled.

“You want some French toast and cheese eggs before you go?” Ms. Turner offered.

“Nah, ma, but make a plate for Junior; he’ll probably eat it when he gets up,” Muffin suggested.

“OK, baby. How long you gon’ be?” Ms. Turner asked.

“I’m gon’ make a full morning out of it. After Bloomies I’m goin’ to the Village to see if I can find me some hot sandals. You know the weather breaking and summer will be here in no time,” Muffin said, smiling.

“OK, baby. Be careful. I love you,” Ms. Turner said, kissing Muffin on the cheek before she left. Muffin left and walked to the corner to flag a cab to take her to the train station downtown.

Junior jumped out of bed having to use the bathroom to relieve himself from all the liquor and beer he consumed with his cousin, Craig, the night before. He urinated what felt like ten minutes then washed his face and brushed his teeth. When he went to get back in bed he noticed Muffin was gone. It was rare she left without letting him know she was stepping out so he figured she was downstairs.

He went downstairs to see what she was doing and could smell the aroma of breakfast cooking; good thoughts of having breakfast in bed danced in his head. He was famished so her making him breakfast was a welcome treat. When he entered the kitchen he almost fell backward when he noticed Muffin’s mother standing at the sink washing dishes. Junior gazed at her beautiful form through the psychedelic satin robe she wore. The fabric outlined

her firm hips and round robust ass as it seemed to clap while she washed the dishes with vigor.

Her hair was wrapped up so the nape of her neck was exposed along with one bare shoulder where the satin robe slightly slipped off from her arm movements. Her right foot was balled up like a fist and rested comfortably on her left foot as she continued to scrub the pot she had made eggs in. The robe reached a little below her thigh and Junior eyed her like she was his last meal. At that moment, she turned around exposing her perky breasts, which were visible from the half-opened robe she was wearing. Startled, she dropped the pot in her hand and attempted to cover herself up with her arms. Junior's eyes were steady and he didn't flinch as he stood his ground and waited for a spoken word. She gathered the house robe by its belt and pulled it around her body trying to conceal her nakedness as she backed up into the sink unconsciously.

Junior moved toward her slowly but with confidence, never breaking eye contact. Every step taken was movement toward something so taboo it would bring an avalanche of hurt feelings and confusion into relationships that were built on love, trust, and honesty. The idea of what could happen once Junior reached his destination was both pleasurable and painful, the latter having a sustaining effect.

When he was within arm's length, Junior reached out slowly to the belt on the robe and held it between his index finger and thumb and pulled it slowly until he could see the knot unravel. There was no resistance so he continued by opening the robe and pulling one side off her shoulders to expose the left side of her body. Her breasts were beautiful to the sight and her thong was filled out superbly with her well-proportioned weight. The other side

of the robe fell on its own and aside from her thong, she was completely naked. Junior knelt slowly, still within arm's reach and without a word, and grabbed her soft thighs, raising one of her legs up and kissing it sensuously. He was careful to take his time because he wanted physical and mental approval. He licked her thigh and sucked it gently as he massaged the other with his free hand. He heard a faint moan being released from somewhere deep inside her voice box.

As his licks got closer to her valley, he could feel slight resistance—not from disapproval, it was more anxiety of satisfaction that made her jerk slightly. His tongue moved her thong to the side and slipped into a heavily saturated cavern that seemed to be dripping with eagerness. He lapped around the inside of her middle and then his tongue found its way up to her hardened clit. He brushed pass it gently and her body shook from the touch. He licked it slowly then increased his pace and suddenly she was grabbing his head with both hands and gyrating her hips, thrusting her pelvic region forward. Her moan became audible and she threw her head back and enjoyed the feeling Junior was giving her. Her eyes were closed and she licked her lips as he sucked her clit until a warm slippery liquid passed from her love hole down his chin.

She shuddered and shook almost losing her footing as she contained the roar she wanted to release from inside her esophagus. Junior peered up at her, wondering if he would be able to finish off what he started without any involuntary resistance. He prepared for the next level and looked up at his mature conquest and saw she was totally enveloped in all he was doing. He stood up and was about to kiss her but decided against it because that move proved too intimate for the violation that was being committed.

Instead, he latched onto her breast and sucked her nipples, which brought increased pleasure to her as she continued to moan like a child who was just punished.

Her nipples hardened in his mouth as he sucked them and peeled her thong down over her thighs. She wiggled her ass to help him get the thongs beyond her hips and stepped out of them when it reached her ankles. Junior's index finger rubbed her clit and spread the sticky juices around her lips like a glazed donut then inserted it inside her hole going in and out slowly, feeling her hips move to his movements. He raised her right leg and placed it on his right forearm and backed her gently up to the kitchen sink and used his left hand to grab his pipe and slide it inside her slippery core.

She winced but invited his entry and nibbled on his ear as he pumped in and out of her snatch slowly. He was well endowed and she was surprised by how full she felt when he entered her. Her entire body was submerged in ecstasy as it had been so long since she had had any sexual relations with the opposite sex. Junior grabbed her by the waist and inserted his full staff into her and she let out a yelp from the pressure. He rotated his hips and grinded himself against her with his head laying on her breasts and his back arched like a dog humping a bitch in heat. Her legs were getting weak and she wanted to collapse on the floor, but the sensation from the friction of his dick to her pussy kept her steady.

Her moaning grew louder as his thrusts increased progressively. His dick was soaked as it slid easily in and out of her. He felt himself about to cum so he slowed his pace to stop himself from busting prematurely. She felt the pulsating in the head of his shaft and she squeezed her vaginal walls and pumped back hard, her thighs and calves

tightening as she pushed herself against him hard, preventing him from pulling out of her.

Junior couldn't contain himself; he felt the eruption coming. He tried to hold back but she pressed him harder and harder and squeezed her walls tighter until he screamed out in ecstasy, releasing a load of hot jizzm inside her. Her pussy was like a suction as she drained every drop of cum out of him, causing him to moan like a wounded animal. He was immobilized for some seconds before he was able to pull out of her. She put her leg down once he ejected himself out of her and stood looking at him. The reality of what they both did came speeding to the forefront of her mind and shame was plastered on her face. She picked up her robe and thong and rushed out of the kitchen without saying a word, leaving Junior standing by the kitchen sink with his limp dick in his hand.

***

Muffin had a hard time opening the front door because she had too many bags in her hand. She put the bags on the ground and freed her hands so she could put the key into the heavy wooden door with the glass panes. She pushed the door open and held it open with her foot as she gathered the bags off the floor then went inside the house. She put the bags in the living room and went into the kitchen to get her something cold to drink. Upon entering the kitchen she was hit with a smell that was undeniable to her nostrils, it was a faint smell but it was definitely the smell of sex. Her heartbeat increased because she was thinking the worst and hoped she was overreacting. She looked around the kitchen in search of something that would explain the smell, something that

would make her suspicions unfounded. There were still dishes in the sink and there was still a frying pan on the stove to be washed from the breakfast that was cooked earlier in the day. She grabbed the bags out of the living room and went upstairs to her room. When she opened the door she heard the shower and peeked inside to find Junior inside the tub.

"Ay, boy." She pulled the curtain back.

"What's up, ma?" he responded, lathering himself up.

"Nothing. Just letting you know I'm back from shopping," she replied, releasing the shower curtain.

"Why didn't you tell me you was going shopping? I woulda went with you," he screamed from the shower.

"I knew you just got in so I didn't want to wake you," she said, picking up his boxers and inspecting them for fresh stains.

There was nothing out of the ordinary and he wasn't acting suspicious, but her intuition wouldn't allow her to dismiss what she was thinking. She sat down on the bed and looked through her bags, separating the items she picked up for Junior. She got up from the bed and walked down the hall to her mother's room and knocked on the door. She didn't get an answer so she pushed the door open and her mother was laying on the bed with the covers over her.

"Ma, you woke?" she whispered from the door. Her mother moaned a little.

"Ma, ma, you woke?" she whispered a little louder.

"Hmm hmm," her mother mumbled.

"I was just letting you know I was back from shopping," Muffin said, closing her bedroom door.

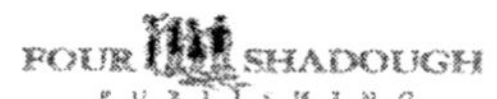

She stood in the hallway and wondered if what she smelled in the kitchen was really what she thought she smelled in the kitchen. She didn't have reason to think something was happening between Junior and her mother but the smell was distinctive and she couldn't shake it from her mind. She was going to watch them both closely and see if she could detect anything. Then her suspicions would be either confirmed or denied.

Junior got out of the shower wondering if Muffin's mother would say anything about what happened. The more he thought about it, the more he felt she wouldn't say anything. If she told, Muffin would be hurt by two people she loved and trusted, but the pain from her mother's betrayal would cause more damage than his own. Satisfied that their secret would be safe and that he and Muffin's relationship would not suffer, he continued on with his plans.

Chapter 16

Chico wasn't making as much money as he was before because La was only giving him small packages until he found out who snitched on him. He said the snitch was going to make all the other workers suffer financially.

The news of Shondra's pregnancy gave Chico a sense of urgency for getting money so he could support his unborn child as well as Shondra. His financial situation needed to change quickly before his child was born. He wanted to prove to her he was ready for a family and could be a good father.

Taylor and Burke pulled up to the curb unbeknownst to Chico, startling him when they got out of the car.

"Hey, Chico. Long time no hear from. What's going on? I see you're still out here working," Taylor said, approaching him slowly.

Chico looked around to make sure no one was out before answering the detectives. "Why y'all come over here like this? That muhfucka already know somebody snitching on him and if he hear I was talking to you then he gon' do something to me. Y'all trying to get me killed?" Chico asked nervously.

"Not at all. We're here to see if we can save you. We've been coming around and haven't seen him. When we saw you we figured you could tell us where he is," Taylor said.

Chico was looking around nervously. "Y'all had him and let him go. I gave y'all all the information you needed to get him and y'all didn't do nothing. Now he know somebody snitching on him so he not coming around until he found out who snitched or until y'all stop looking for him. I think he already suspects I snitched and me talking with y'all is all the proof he gon' need," Chico cried out in a low voice.

"Well, technically, you are, but that's beside the point of why we're here. We need to find out if you know the whereabouts of La or Junior. We'll take either one," Taylor said.

"Y'all don't give a fuck about what happens to me if that muhfucka finds out I'm the one that told. I don't know where he at and I don't know where Junior at either, so please leave me alone," Chico begged.

"Oh, we won't be leaving you alone until we get what we want—unless you plan to stop selling that shit you have in your pockets. The only reason we're not taking you in right now is because you've been cooperative. But once you stop, you will be going down on possession and sale charges. Why don't you be a good informant and try and get that information to us. *Unless you're quitting today*," Taylor patted him on his shoulder as Chico tried to move away.

Taylor and Burke walked back to their car. Chico scanned the area to see if anyone witnessed his unscheduled meeting with the police. There were only a

few older people walking past the building but he didn't see anyone who could threaten to reveal his secret.

***

La's fists were clenched. Although he believed Chico would stay loyal to him out of fear, he had suspicions that he was the one who snitched on him. He planned on killing Chico the day he called and begged for work but waited because he wanted to get something solid on him that would prove his suspicions. La hit him with a package that was just enough for him to hustle and not give out to the other workers. He secretly watched Chico everyday while he sold off the pack. Then La would hit him with more when he was finished.

As La noted, Chico's routine rarely changed from going to Shondra's house for a spell then back to his building afterward. La was beginning to believe he was wrong about Chico until he saw the same two detectives from the day he was questioned jump out on Chico. At first he thought they were going to bust Chico for a sale but they never checked for contraband; instead they held what seemed like a hearty conversation with Chico, who kept looking around nervously like he was afraid someone would see him talking to them. While they talked La wished he could hear exactly what they were saying. However, seeing Chico's reaction to the detectives was all the proof he needed. When they left, he was so mad he wanted to run up to Chico and put two bullets in his head. He decided against it. He was going to make the young rat suffer the death of a snitch so everyone who found out about it would know that snitching was not tolerated on his

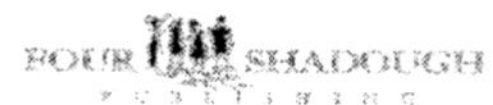

team. Chico was marked for death and La put the bullseye on his back for accuracy.

***

Every time La stopped at a red light, he clutched the handle of his pistol and looked to his left and right before the light turned green. He was more paranoid lately because he was so anxious to get rid of Chico. It had been a week since the incident with the detectives and he was on his way to Baptiste to pick up the rest of his money. Then, he resolved, he was going to end Chico's worthless life. He felt he was doing the hood a favor by getting rid of a snitch. He kept the hammer in his lap because he had to be wary of the detectives and his ongoing beef with Junior. Both posed a threat and he planned on taking out either one without a worry of the consequences. It was better to be safe than sorry—he learned that when he got shot—and he would be damned if he got caught unarmed again.

Once he finished Chico, he was going to pick Shondra's brain to find out if she still harbored any hatred toward Junior and see if he could get a location on him. As long as Junior was alive and loose on the streets, he had to watch his back everywhere he went.

He continued driving down Lafayette Avenue shaking his head at the thought of Chico thinking he could outsmart him. It infuriated him because he gave the young boy a chance after he stole from him. Then he turns around and snitches on him.

La was the boss in Baptiste, he was making major bread, and single-handedly dismantled Junior's team and took over his spot. He laid down his murder game and was a powerful man in the hood. He was about his money,

always on point and felt he was untouchable. His ego had him believing Junior was afraid of him and the detectives couldn't get him, even with help from the snitch. To have a young, pussy-like Chico try and take him out the game brought blood to his eyes. He was going to make the young boy suffer a terrible death and enjoy doing it and then he would slowly get his operation running full steam again. None of the other workers would even think about talking to the police after hearing what had happened to Chico.

La pulled over to a bodega on Myrtle Avenue next to Fort Greene Park and went inside to purchase a blunt and a cold beer. He walked to the back of the store and opened the glass freezer door and grabbed a 40 oz. of Colt 45 and went back toward the counter. When he reached the counter, the front door of the store opened and a beautiful girl walked inside. She was dressed in a form-fitting, black stretch skirt that stopped short of her hips, showing her thick butterscotch thighs. She complimented it with knee-high hooker boots and a bustier that made her breasts seem much larger than they really were. The Louie shoulder bag she was carrying in her hand hung gracefully as she sashayed inside. She caught La's attention immediately as she walked to the counter and stared in his eyes momentarily. She produced a seductive smile.

" 'Scuse me, love," she said to La, taking his place in line.

"No, excuse me, hun," La said, backing up and letting her get in front of him so he could see her ass.

"Let me get two Phillies," she told the Latino man behind the counter.

"I see somebody 'bout to get right," La said to her.

"And you know that's right. I'm 'bout to get my head tight, baby," she said, turning around to speak to La directly.

"I wish I could join that party," La said, looking into her chinky eyes.

"I don't know, babes, maybe we can make that happen. What you gettin' into tonight?" she asked in her high-pitched voice, taking the blunts off the counter.

"Hopefully you," La said, placing his beer on the counter and pulling out a wad of money to show he was caked up.

"Hmmm. Seems like you holdin', daddy. Any of that got my name on it?" She asked, looking at the wad of bills he was peeling to pay for his items.

"Sure do, hun. 'Specially if your last name is Grant," he said, waving a fifty dollar bill.

"Grant is my maiden name, love; my married name is Franklin," she replied sassily.

"I heard that! Well, I have all the relatives to go along with him. Why don't you give me a number so we can hook up and get better acquainted?" La licked his lips.

He usually didn't pay for pussy but if she wanted some money, he was going to give it to her—but only this once. The only thing he liked about females like her was not having to worry about any attachment afterward. Spending money up front just guaranteed he was fucking and he liked the odds.

"Oh, you talking 'bout hangin' later on? What's wrong with right now? I mean, unless you have something more important to do…" She turned around and rubbed her ass and shook it as she exited the store.

La was turned on and didn't want to miss out on the opportunity, so he hurried outside to see if he could get

something going with her immediately. He could postpone what he was going to do to Chico because his fate was already sealed as far as he was concerned, so there was no rush.

“Hold up, hun. What you talkin’ ‘bout doin’? I want to make sure we on the same page before I commit myself to anything, you feel me?” La said, getting to the point.

“It’s whatever, baby. You can come chill at my spot or we can go where you feel like taking me. I feel safe wherever I go. I can handle myself,” she said with confidence.

“Aight, I’m feeling that. You walking or you whipping?” Las asked her, following her as she walked around the corner from the store.

“I’m walking,” she said, intentionally shaking her ass hard.

“Why don’t you ride with me and we’ll stop and get some chow real quick then head over to the telly right quick so we can get this party poppin’,” La propositioned.

“Sounds like a plan to me. I hope you not talking about one of those rat-infested, four-hour motels with the cigarette burns in the sheets, ‘cause if you are, I’m gonna have to take a rain check, daddy. I might be fast but I’m no slow leak. And while we on the subject, I need my money up front if I’m riding wit’ you. You feel me?” Her attitude changed from pleasant to straight business.

La was digging her style; this was the kind of female he would want to keep around. He was going to try and keep her around by playing her the right way.

“No question, baby. Let’s walk over to my car and let’s make it happen,” La said, leading her to where he parked his car.

The black Maxima was parked in the middle of the block across the street from Fort Greene Park. As the couple strolled, La was engaged in small talk with his lady friend and couldn't get over how lucky he was to have encountered her while stopping in the store to get his beer. The block was pretty much deserted aside from the occasional bike rider riding through the tree-lined streets.

La was engrossed in his conversation with the girl as they headed to his car. He heard a loud clicking noise that broke his concentration with his lady friend.

"What the fuck!" he screamed as he noticed a figure standing near his car.

"Wait!" Muffin screamed, when she saw La pull his gun from his waist heading toward his car, shooting in the direction of the unidentified figure.

Junior ducked for cover as he heard the gunfire coming from La. He moved into the street and peeped through car windows he passed, hoping Muffin would take care of her target before he reached him.

Muffin was frozen with fear as she watched La shooting at Junior and couldn't move.

La turned his attention to Muffin momentarily to tell her to get low but the boom from Junior's gun stopped his thoughts and he turned around and fired his weapon in Junior's direction again; Junior ducked behind a car.

"Come on, muhfucka!" La screamed.

Junior could see faces in the windows of residents who were alarmed after hearing the gunshots. He knew they probably called the police so he had to get rid of La quickly. He rose to his feet and let off three shots.

Muffin pulled out the handgun and walked up to La, who was stooping down behind a car for cover. He didn't notice the gun in her hand when he turned around and told

her, "Get down!" Suddenly, he felt a searing pain in his shoulder that knocked him to the ground and forced him to drop his gun. Muffin pointed her gun at him as he lay on the ground, closed her eyes, and squeezed off more shots. The gun jerked in her hand and when she opened her eyes she had clearly missed because he was going for his gun. She freaked out and backed up squeezing the trigger but lost her balance and fell to the hard concrete. Her gun flew out of her hand as she watched La struggle to his feet then point his gun in her direction.

"You set me up, bitch!" He couldn't believe he got played. Junior definitely caught him slipping but he wasn't going to let him win, he was about to level the playing field by silencing the bitch then ending Junior's life right after.

Muffin was trying to get to her gun and turned white with fear, looking into the black hole of the gun La had pointed at her. She didn't want to believe what was about to happen to her. She turned her face away and wailed uncontrollably. She braced herself for the end and let out an ear-piercing scream when she heard the blast from the gun.

Everything was quiet and still except for the sirens blaring from the police cars racing to the carnage. Junior kneeled down and grabbed Muffin around her waist and pulled her to her feet. She was limp in his arms as he struggled with her to stand up.

Junior witnessed Muffin walking up to La and when he heard the first shot ring out, he ran from the where he was hiding across the street and crept up behind La. When she squeezed off again, La crawled to get his gun and got up to shoot Muffin but never saw Junior standing

behind him. When he was upright, Junior shot him in the back of his head before he could get his shot off.

Muffin was on the ground like a leaf when Junior tried to steady her so she could regain her balance. Then she looked at La lying on the ground. She saw his arm and leg jerk then she bent down and picked up the gun she dropped when she fell backward trying to get away from him.

"You stupid muhfucka!" she screamed as tears streamed down her face. "You was gonna kill me!" She pulled the trigger repeatedly until the gun was empty.

Junior looked at Muffin and was shocked to see her kill La with such fierceness.

"Come on, Muff, we gotta get the fuck outta here!" he told her.

His voice and the sounds of the sirens brought her back to reality. "Where's the car?" she asked.

"Around the corner. Come on before someone IDs us," Junior said, walking quickly to the corner.

Muffin followed behind him with her head lowered, unaware she was still holding the weapon she used to finish La off. When Junior turned and saw she still had the gun, he immediately stopped.

"Give me that, Muff," he said, grabbing the weapon with his gloved hand.

Muffin got into the passenger seat of the Jeep and Junior jumped in the driver's side looking around carefully to make sure no one saw what vehicle they entered then inserted the key in the ignition and pulled off slowly into traffic, passing oncoming police cars with blaring sirens. He looked over at Muffin and she looked liked she was in temporary shock: her eyes were fixed on nothing in particular and she wasn't blinking. He placed her gun

under the backseat and removed his rubber glove then gently grabbed her hand.

Muffin proved to be a valuable asset to him. Although he loved her, he had to look out for his well-being first. After Shondra snitched on him, he realized the love she had for him really held no weight and was pushed to the side when she found out about his affair with Muffin. That proved to him that love could be compromised.

When he fucked Muffin's mother, he knew that was the ultimate betrayal and if Muffin ever found out, she would never forgive him. Her anger about that alone could also compromise their relationship and her loyalty and she could go to the police and give him up in the murder of her cousin Drez. He couldn't risk that happening so he had to think smart and the gun on the floor was his ace in the hole. He had no intention of using it unless he was forced to but he was going to keep it as leverage if she ever threatened him with jail. He would make sure she was aware she too would be going away for murder, no questions asked. Until then, he was going to love her and make sure she was ok.

"I think we need to take this trip back to North Carolina and lay low for a while. What you think Muff?" he asked her.

"Yea, baby, I'm ready to get the fuck away from New York," Muffin said, leaning her head against the window.

Chapter 17
K.B. & Gloria

K.B. and Gloria closed on the house and were preparing to move in within the month. Gloria was excited because K.B. surprised her with the purchase, which was a much-needed boost of confidence to let her know he was still in love with her. After the ass kicking she took at the barbershop, she wanted Patricia fired. However, K.B. insisted she stay only because he promised they would be opening another barbershop close to where they bought their house and then he would relocate Patricia to the new location and have someone else manage it. Gloria wasn't happy with his suggestion because she still had to see her whenever she went to that location to take care of the books. Since having the fight with Patricia, K.B. always accompanied her to the barbershop and left together to make sure nothing else jumped off. That was the only upside to the altercation she had with Patricia: K.B. was always with her and that made her feel more secure in their relationship. They had become inseparable, which helped dispel the rumors that he and Patricia were seeing each other on the low.

K.B. was trying his best to keep the peace in his barbershop. He didn't want his girl to be unhappy but

didn't want Patricia unhappy either. He was out of pocket for feeling the way he did for Patricia, but it was genuine. Her youth and innocence, not to mention her slamming body, were the main attractions that had him desperately wanting to get between her sugar walls. He told Gloria that Patricia would work at the other shop they planned on opening; he told Patricia a different story. Patricia understood that she would be running that shop as if it were her own and Gloria wasn't going to have anything to do with it: it was going to be unisex and there would be a general manager to take care of everything. All Gloria would be required to do is go over the monthly books to make sure everything was right.

K.B. and Gloria pulled up in front of the shop; Gloria entered the shop first. Everyone greeted her and she responded in kind, except for Patricia, who didn't acknowledge her presence anyway. She only peeked up to see who was coming through the door then went back to doing her client's hair. When K.B. entered everyone gave a hearty greeting and he, too, responded in kind. When Patricia saw him, however, she lit up like a beacon and spoke lovingly.

"Hey, Keith, how are you this afternoon? You starting to come in later and later, I see," she said, batting her eyes.

"Heh, heh. I'm good, Pat. I have some other business I have to take care of so that's why I been late coming to the shop," he replied, admiring her voluptuous body.

Gloria was already in the office so she was out of earshot to the obvious flirting going on between K.B. and Patricia. Patricia looked him up and down. It would only

be a matter of time before she actually gave in to K.B. and let him sample her goodies. If only she were able to take him completely away from that black-ass Gloria.

Junior & Muffin

Junior and Muffin had been back down south for some weeks and were enjoying themselves. Junior's cousin, Bo, was making so much money they became kingpins in the town. They branched out and had the surrounding towns copping weight from them like the Dominicans on Broadway. Junior had become boss in this small town and was feeling good about the way things were going. He was at the top of his game and had taken care of one of the major loose ends he had by laying his murder game down in New York. The only thing he had to worry about was having a warrant for his arrest for the murder of Muffin's cousin, Drez, thanks to Shondra. He was no longer worried about Muffin flipping on him about the murder of her cousin Drez because he had a murder weapon with her fingerprints all over it. He had rock-solid insurance that she would keep her mouth shut.

Everything was looking good and going in Junior's favor so he was somewhat at peace. He looked over at Muffin and brought her close to him and looked into her eyes.

Muffin looked up into his eyes, knowing she was with a thorough man. When he told her his plan to murder La, he had asked her would she participate because he knew of La's weakness for females. He banked on La not thinking a female would be capable of setting him up. At first, she was hesitant because it involved her directly. She was afraid of getting hurt or killed if the plan didn't go off

well. He convinced her by explaining the element of surprise and how it would be on their side. And, he added, by the time La figured out what was happening it would be too late; his brains would be splattered all over the sidewalk. She agreed and was ready but when it happened, she missed her target because she closed her eyes and thought her life was over when she was staring down the barrel of La's gun. She choked. She cursed Junior in those few seconds but then remembered she agreed to do it and had to be ready to accept her fate. She was all but ready to give up but Junior kept his word and he killed La and saved her life. From that day forward, she knew she could trust him with her life. She was not afraid to ride or die with him.

"Hey, Bo?" Junior called out to his cousin, who was sitting next to the couple counting money.

"What is it, cuzzin'?" Bo looked up from counting.

"I want to take the day—me and my baby—and just pamper our self. You know what I mean?" Junior said to him.

"Not directly. Whatcha wanna do?" Bo asked.

"I want to take my boo to get her hair done and I want to get a fresh cut. Then I want to go shopping, get dressed, jump on the highway, and go to another town. And while we're there, I want to see if I can drum up some more business. You feel me?" Junior explained.

Bo laid out an itinerary. "OK, I hear you, cuz. First off, you kin go the barbershop on the Block; they have barbers and a girl that does hair, so y'all both can go and get did up at the same place. After that we can ride out to Greenville and hit the mall. As far as business, I think you might like Raleigh. It's a nice ride from o'er here and I

reckon you can meet some folk there that would be interested in what you selling."

Sounds like a plan. What you think, Muff?" Junior asked, looking at her as her head rested on his shoulder.

"It sounds good to me, baby," Muffin replied.

Junior's pager went off and when he looked at it he turned to Bo and told him to get a big eighth ready.

"Aight, Muff, we gon' drop you off at the barbershop so you can get your hair done and after me and Bo take care of this business, I'll come to get my hair cut. From there, we'll head to the mall in Greenville," Junior told her.

"OK, daddy," Muffin said, getting herself ready.

Junior and Bo dropped Muffin at New York Kutz then pulled off to go handle their business. Muffin walked into the shop. When the bell rang everyone's attention was on her. She walked past the three barbers and went over to Patricia's station.

"Hi, do I need to make an appointment to get my hair done?" she asked.

"You sho' don't, honey. I have one more head to do and you can be right after her if you don't mind waiting," Patricia responded in a sweet tone.

"How long is the wait?" Muffin asked, looking around the shop.

"I'm almost done with her and my next client only wants a wash and set so it should only be twenty minutes to a half hour, OK?" Patricia told her.

Muffin looked at the client's hair then replied, "OK, as long as it don't turn into a whole hour."

"Oh, I promise you it ain't gon' take no hour 'fore I see you," Patricia said, checking Muffin out.

Muffin nodded her head and took a seat in one of the empty chairs then picked up a magazine and started leafing through it.

Patricia could tell that her new customer was from up north by her accent and by her stylish apparel. She was really pretty with beautiful hair and had an air of confidence that beamed when she walked into the shop.

Gloria came out of the back office and walked past Patricia and glanced over to where Muffin was sitting. Immediately, she recognized her and rushed over to confirm her identity.

"Oh shit! What's up, girl?" Gloria screamed.

Muffin looked up from her magazine, startled and shocked to see Gloria standing in front of her.

"Oh my God! Hey, girl. What you doin' down here?" Muffin said, standing up to hug a familiar face in a foreign town.

"Working. You know this is me and my boo's barbershop. We been down here almost a year now," Gloria said proudly.

"Wow. This is really nice. I shoulda known when I came in 'cause I can see y'all gave it that Brooklyn feel," Muffin said, looking around, admiring the decor.

"Yea, girl, I miss the hell outta New York. This country shit gets corny at times," Gloria remarked, rolling her eyes at Patricia, who was eyeing both women.

Muffin immediately recognized the obvious tension between both women but refrained from making any acknowledgement because she didn't want to get pulled into any beef.

"So…how long the barbershop been open?" Muffin asked, sidestepping Gloria's earlier remark.

"It's been open about ten months now, I think. We almost making a year as business owners!" Gloria calculated. "So what brings you down here to the boondocks? I didn't even know this part of North Carolina was on the map, so you know I'm shocked to see anybody from Brooklyn stroll in. Especially someone I know!"

Before Muffin could think of a lie, the doorbell chimed again and everyone in the barbershop turned their attention to the figure walking through the door. Gloria gasped as Junior walked into the shop. He strolled past some of the patrons and slapped most of them five and made his way to Muffin. Gloria was already shocked to see Junior but her jaw dropped when he kissed Muffin on her cheek. Gloria looked at Muffin and then at Junior, who just noticed her standing there.

"He the one you was talking about when you was fighting Shondra? You…you was fucking her man?" Gloria managed to say.

"Yea, so what bitch!" Junior answered wickedly, staring daggers at Gloria.

The patrons in the barbershop could sense something was wrong and anxiously waited for something to pop off. Patricia looked at Gloria and could see the fear written all over her face. She also noticed Muffin looking uncomfortable as well and figured the guy who came into the barbershop was the cause for all the worried looks on the faces of both women. She was curious to know what was going on along with everyone else in the shop. Then K.B. walked out from the office and it all became clear.

When Junior noticed K.B. coming from somewhere in the back of the barbershop he quickly shifted his icy glare to him. K.B. stopped midway when he realized it was Junior standing in his barbershop. He scanned the shop and

his eyes landed on Muffin and he immediately caught a flashback of the night he was shot in the club. Then with a pointed finger he blurted out, "That's the bitch that shot me!"

"And she shoulda killed your ass," Junior hissed.

Both men stared at each other, no one making any quick movements. While both men were preoccupied face-fighting one another, Gloria looked at Muffin and hate consumed her. She impulsively lunged at Muffin. Muffin knew what time it was and dived forward too and they both crashed into each other with enormous force. Gloria was screaming at the top of her lungs. "You shot my man, bitch! You played me! I shoulda let Shondra whip your ass!" Muffin tuned out whatever Gloria was saying and concentrated on the blows she delivered to Gloria's jaw. Muffin grabbed her by her hair and swung her around and they both fell into the chairs. Gloria grabbed onto Muffin's shirt and head-butted her. They both were swinging wildly, periodically connecting with some of their blows. Muffin shifted her weight and used her elbows and slammed them against Gloria's face in a sweeping motion, sending her tumbling backward. Muffin got up and jumped at Gloria but Junior grabbed her by the back of her shirt and pulled her to him. K.B. grabbed Gloria and spun her around so she was facing him, then gently moved her to the side.

Junior and K.B. stood their ground until Junior spoke. "Small world, huh, muhfucka. You musta thought you could hide out by coming to this small-ass town."

"Nah, you got me fucked up. I ain't hiding from shit. I'm here for business," K.B. replied.

"What a coincidence! I'm here for business, too, and from how I see it, this town ain't big enough for the both of us." Junior kept his eyes glued to K.B.

"I think you mixed up. My business is not the same as yours. I own this barbershop," K.B. clarified.

"Who gives a fuck!" Junior bellowed.

Muffin looked at Gloria and then at K.B. and slowly moved closer to the entrance of the barbershop. No one else moved.

K.B. was frozen; his past had come back to haunt him. There was still unfinished business in New York and it came to North Carolina looking for him. He met Junior's stare and he could see death in the man's eyes. He was approximately 100 feet away and the only thing separating them were the patrons, barber chairs, and a thick fog of hate permeating the atmosphere. The stillness in the barbershop was nerve-wracking; the only sound was the low humming coming from the barbers' clippers, everyone was waiting nervously for something to happen.

Once Muffin was standing next to the door, Junior told her to leave the shop and get in the car. The bell dinged as she opened the door but Junior never broke the glare fixed on K.B. K.B. whispered something to Gloria and she quickly went into the office. The door dinged again and Bo walked into the barbershop. Some of the patrons recognized him.

"E'erything awright in here, cuzzin'? Your old lady said there might be a problem up in here. You need this?" Bo asked, producing a massive, long-barreled .357. He passed it to Junior.

Junior took it out of his hands quickly and pointed it in K.B.'s direction. Upon seeing the gun, the barbershop broke out in a panic and the patrons and the barbers ducked trying to avoid becoming a casualty of the feud, should Junior have decided to start firing.

Gloria had come out of the office and passed K.B. the gun that was always left inside the shop in the event of a robbery. That was precisely when Bo came into the barbershop and passed Junior his gun. K.B. grabbed the gun in his hand and both men were standing in the shop pointing guns at each other. The air was thick with anxiety. No one dared moved in the barbershop, afraid any sudden movement would prompt an eruption of gunfire. The shop was too small for the enormous beef between both men.

Junior was boiling with anger when he saw Gloria pass K.B. the gun but it was too late. His hand was steady as he kept the pistol focused on K.B., but he was not too happy with the way things were playing out.

"How you want to do this, muhfucka!" Junior screamed, not caring about anything at the moment.

"However you want it, bitch nigga!" K.B. shoved Gloria into the office. "Go in the office Glo!"

Junior pulled the trigger of his magnum and K.B. let his automatic go. The deafening and deadly sound of gunfire rang out. Then, as fast as the gunfire started, it stopped.

Muffin came running into the barbershop, now filled with smoke, and Gloria came running out of the office. The strong smell of gunpowder violated both women nostrils and they both screamed out in unison when they saw bodies lying on the ground. All the barbers and patrons jumped up and rushed out the barbershop, some screaming while others shoved, trying to escape to safety. There was no movement after everyone vacated the barbershop except for the two women who were kneeling down beside the wounded bodies. They both rubbed the hands of the men on the ground and looked up to the